Outplayed

Era Capoeira, Volume 3

Shonel Jackson

Published by Shonel Jackson, 2025.

This is a work of fiction. Similarities to real people, places, or events are entirely coincidental.

OUTPLAYED

First edition. April 16, 2025.

Copyright © 2025 Shonel Jackson.

ISBN: 978-1739252199

Written by Shonel Jackson.

Also by Shonel Jackson

Era Capoeira
Let's Play
Playing With Fire
Outplayed

Standalone
Let's Play
Playing With Fire

Watch for more at https://www.shoneljackson.com/.

Table of Contents

CHAPTER 1 1
CHAPTER 2 14
CHAPTER 3 34
CHAPTER 4 56
CHAPTER 5 66
CHAPTER 6 78
CHAPTER 7 97
CHAPTER 8 115
CHAPTER 9 129
CHAPTER 10 147
CHAPTER 11 160
CHAPTER 12 174
CHAPTER 13 189
CHAPTER 14 202
EPILOGUE 231

I dedicate this book to *Capoeira Ceará*, and especially to *Mestre Caboclin*. Playing *Capoeira* at this school was a landmark period of my life and lessons I learned there have stayed with me to this day. *Jogo bonito!*

CHAPTER 1

- ginga -

Dominic Made sat on a barstool nursing his second glass of bourbon. He was not having a good day. In fact, his entire week hadn't been anything to write home about. The absolute last place he wanted to be tonight was out in public. However, even in his present state of mind, he knew that drinking copious amounts of alcohol alone in his apartment probably wouldn't be healthy. The bar was full, but right now he felt like he only had his glass of bourbon for company. Besides, he needed to be here. Tonight, that was his lot in life, so he just sat there and kept on sipping.

Dominic had been sitting there on the short end of the 'L' shaped bar for almost an hour and had barely looked up since he'd got there. His eyes had been firmly fixed on the swirl of brown liquid in his glass. However, some invisible force was making him raise his gaze now. There was a woman sitting at the bar a few metres away from him. She was looking straight ahead and Dominic thought she was probably staring at her reflection in the mirror behind the bar. Her back was straight, her neck was long and her skin looked like smooth milk chocolate. All his life, Dominic had had a type, and this woman was definitely it.

The dark, strappy top she wore showed off her elegant shoulders. He watched as she gracefully lifted her glass of white wine and planted red lips around the rim. She took a sip and he saw her chest rise and fall as she savoured the cold liquid making its way down her throat. It was at that moment that Dominic felt a stirring down below.

Fuck! Where the hell had she come from?

He'd been resigned to his current state of grumpiness and now this woman had come out of nowhere to make him horny. He was incredulous.

For fuck's sake!

Try as he might, he couldn't drag his eyes off her. He watched as her jaw tightened and her lips pursed. He'd never seen the woman before in his life, but he would bet anything that she was in almost as bad a mood as he was in right now. Her gaze almost never left the back of the bar and she only looked down whenever she picked up her glass.

He was half tempted to get up, go over there and see if he could turn her frown upside down. He didn't do that, of course. She was hot, but his current mood made him unfit for human company, especially of the hot woman variety.

So instead, he brought his gaze back down and took another sip of his bourbon. He didn't look up again until something in his peripheral vision pulled his attention. The *thing* was in fact a person... a drunk person, to be precise. Central London on a Friday night heaved with them. There was nothing special about this one, except for one thing. He'd placed himself on the stool next to the woman who was very

OUTPLAYED

much Dominic's type, as that barstool had just been vacated by its previous occupant. The drunk was making eyes at her and his intentions were written all over his inebriated face. From what Dominic could see, the woman was paying the drunk zero attention. Then, the drunk fully turned in his stool, faced her and started talking at her. Not talking *to* her, but *at* her. Dominic wasn't close enough to hear what was being said, but he thought he could make a good guess.

The woman, as she had been doing before, kept her gaze forward at all times. The drunk clearly didn't appreciate that, so he tried another tactic. Dominic watched him raise his index finger and place it on her arm, which had been resting on the bar. Without even turning her head to look at him, she took her free hand, lifted his offending finger and dropped it off to the side.

Dominic's eyes widened in shock. Never before had he seen someone react like that to being pestered by a drunk. This woman was clearly a smooth operator, with nerves of steel, who was not easily flustered. His curiosity about her increased tenfold.

The drunk persevered. He lifted his arm and placed it around her shoulders. It was at that point that the woman spun smoothly the other way, away from the drunk, and gracefully got to her feet, taking her glass of wine with her.

How did she move like that? Effortless!

The woman walked away from the bar and headed in the direction of the large fish tank by the window. She continued to sip on her wine and this time, it was the fish in front of her that held her attention.

Lucky fish!

Now that she was standing, Dominic could see that she had very long, shapely legs and a svelte figure. Her legs looked toned beneath the skin-tight, dark trousers she wore. For the first time, he wondered why she was here alone, because she was most definitely here alone. No one expecting company acted like she had. Everything about her oozed sex appeal, from the way her shoulder-length hair framed her beautiful face, to the perfect curve of her tight arse and the graceful way she poured that wine down her throat. Once again, Dominic felt his groin come to life.

It seemed the woman had acquired something of a stalker. The drunk, unperturbed by her previous blow off, walked over to where she now was on his unsteady feet. It was at this point that Dominic realised that he might have to take a short break from his barstool of misery and handle this guy. The last thing he wanted tonight was to interact with anyone he didn't absolutely have to interact with, but his conscience would never let him just sit there while someone was being harassed. In the mood he was in, however, the drunk had better pray that Dominic could control himself if he made Dominic have to get up off his stool.

The drunk went straight up to her and grabbed her arse with one of his filthy hands. She spun around on instinct and sloshed her drink all over the drunk. The woman's beautiful face screwed up in anger. He wasn't sure if she was more pissed that he dared put his hand on her or that he'd made her put her drink in any place other than into her mouth. Either way, Dominic put his nearly empty glass of bourbon down on the bar as he swung around and placed one foot on the floor. He took a deep breath and was prepared to lift himself to his full six feet of height. But before he could, he watched as the woman put her now empty glass on the tray of a passing waiter as she grabbed the drunk by the scruff of his shirt and pulled him in closer to her. She towered over him, and her expression grew menacing. She said something to him and then shoved him away. The drunk nearly fell over.

Dominic stilled his movement. He started to wonder if she actually needed his assistance after all. The sexy woman showed no fear as she appeared to threaten her pest. Dominic thought that surely that would be the end of it. The drunk had been given fair warning that she would not take his shit and that he could go drown himself in another pint of beer, right?

Right?

When the man regained his balance, he still hadn't learned his lesson, however. He instead launched himself at the beauty and this time his face was furious. Without hesitation this time, Dominic rose to his feet, thinking that it was time he put an end to this. The situation looked like it was about to get out of hand. Dominic had spent his life training in a number of hand-to-hand combat skills, but he knew that he wouldn't need to employ even a fifth of any of them to get this piece of crap out of the bar. He'd barely taken two steps when he saw the drunk point his index finger at her. It was inches away from the woman's face.

'*Fucking bitch!*' the drunk sputtered loudly, drawing the attention of several of the patrons. 'Who the *fuck* do you think you are? You think you're too good for me?' He spat as he spoke and slurred his words.

SHONEL JACKSON

She spoke then and though Dominic couldn't hear her, as her voice was so low compared to the ambient noise of the bar, he could read her red lips.

'*Yes.*'

By Dominic's fifth and sixth steps, he watched in utter shock as the woman grabbed the drunk's arm and executed a series of movements. She grabbed his hand and twisted it at the wrist, which caused the man to wince in pain. Then, she brought the same arm around to his back and pushed it upwards. She then put her free arm around the drunk's neck and whispered something in his ear.

He'd seen this move executed a number of times in Hollywood movies and also in some of his combat classes. But he'd never before seen it performed by a sexy woman with red lips, a long, beautiful neck and a body to die for. It was clear now that there was more to this woman than met the eye.

She doesn't need me at all, does she?

Dominic stopped in his tracks on the sidelines of the altercation. The wicked side of him wanted to see how this would play out. From his new vantage point, Dominic could see a tattoo on her upper arm. It was of a snake.

What is that? A python?

The woman pushed the man away from her one last time and went to walk away. She clearly thought her work there was done. How wrong she was... In one last ditch effort to prove that he was a 'man', the drunk came at her again.

'*What a fucking c—*' he slurred.

He never got a chance to finish his disgusting expletive as she'd heard him coming. She glanced at him over her shoulder and then quickly turned around. She brought a bent right leg up and launched her flexed, flat foot straight at the drunk's chest. He looked stunned as he stumbled back.

Definitely not just a pretty face.

The drunk must have had a screw loose, because he came back for more. This would be the last time, however. Within seconds, after another strike from the beauty, the drunk was flat on the ground, inhaling the dust off the floor. He showed no movement except for the occasional twitch. The other patrons, who had witnessed the entire thing, then erupted into spontaneous applause.

How he'd ended up face down was a sight to behold. Dominic was proficient in Jujitsu, Taekwondo and Krav Maga. He'd also dabbled in a few other types of martial arts. Without a shadow of a doubt, the way she'd just executed that spinning kick, which had landed the drunk flat out on his face, proved that she was a highly skilled fighter herself. The drunk had definitely barked up the wrong, beautiful tree tonight.

Is it wrong that watching her drop that drunk turned me on?

Dominic spun back around to the bar and spoke to the bartender. 'Jamal, pour me another glass of whatever *she*,' Dominic indicated the woman, 'was having.'

Jamal nodded, picked up a bottle of Sauvignon Blanc and poured a glass. Dominic took it and walked over to where the drop-dead gorgeous force-to-be-reckoned-with was still standing, stepping over the drunk on his way. He held the glass out to her. She was not as tall as him, but she was pretty darn tall for a woman.

'Here. I believe yours got spilt,' Dominic said.

The woman looked up and her beautiful dark-brown eyes met his grey ones.

If he'd dropped down dead right now on the floor next to the drunk, Dominic would have thought his life was well lived. Observing her from across the bar had been enough to turn him on. Now, standing inches away from her, his groin went into overdrive. He was glad that the lighting in the bar was low and that his trousers were black.

Without a word, she took the glass from him and brought it to her red lips. Even as she sipped, she did not take her eyes off of his. Her gaze was dark, sultry and enticing.

Fuck me! I've died and gone to heaven!

She lowered the glass but not her eyes. 'Thanks.'

Her voice was like silk. Dominic's hard-on couldn't take it anymore, so he knew he had to be the one to look away first. He did the first thing that he could think of. He turned around and looked down at the drunk, still lying on the floor. He pulled a walkie-talkie out of his back pocket, pressed the button on the side and spoke into it.

'Tony, where the hell are you?'

A crackling sound came through the device, followed by a reply. 'I'm just outside having a smoke.'

'You don't get paid to have a smoke in the middle of your shift. Get your arse in here. Now!' It was shit like this that really pissed Dominic off.

'Sure, Dom,' said Tony, a slight tremor in his voice.

'Hurry up!' Dominic added. 'There's some garbage in here that needs to be taken out.'

'Sure thing, boss.'

Dominic placed the device back into his pocket. Then he turned back to the woman still standing behind him, sipping on her white wine.

OUTPLAYED

'You alright?' Dominic asked.

She nodded, a smirk forming on her lips.

'Where did you learn that kick? Karate? Muay Thai?'

The woman's eyebrow rose. 'Capoeira.'

'Ahh...'

Colour me impressed!

Dominic took the opportunity, now that he was finally this close to her, to fully take her in. Her face was perfect. He loved her bone structure. All he wanted to do was run his finger along her cheek bones and down her long, swan-like neck. He didn't dare, however, as she'd probably try to drop him like she'd just done to the drunk.

Instead, he let his eyes do the touching, being careful not to let it look too obvious that he was memorising every inch of her body.

'Nice tattoo,' he said. 'What is it? A python?'

She gave him a sly smile. Her eyes shone with mischief. 'No. A viper.'

Later, Dominic cast his eyes around the bar. It was now empty and clean. All of his staff had left twenty minutes ago. He'd supervised the clean-up, done the end-of-shift paperwork and locked the day's takings in the safe.

It was late, nearly three in the morning. He wanted to go jump on his bike and take a ride to clear his head. His apartment was above the bar, so he only needed to ride as far as his mood took him, keeping in mind the return journey. However, he lingered. First, he looked at the barstool she'd sat on, then brought his eyes up to the spot on the mirror at the back of his bar that she must have been looking at. Four glass shelves ran along the expanse of the mirror and they were filled with an array of wines, spirits and liqueurs. There was something for every budget. Dominic was a bourbon man himself. Though, the bottle of his preferred bourbon brand was not kept on those shelves. Jamal and his other bartenders knew to keep his bottle of twenty-six-year-old Glenfiddich in a locked cabinet under the bar.

He turned on his heel and brought his eyes to the two-metre-wide fish tank. Admittedly, it had been an extravagance. Dominic's sister, Joy, had insisted that it would add to the ambiance of his bar, so he'd listened to her and invested in the giant tank. Joy had then completed the look with multiple, multi-coloured tropical fish. He had to admit that he did like the thing. Joy was right. But after tonight, he liked it even more, because it was what had drawn in his Capoeira beauty as she'd attempted to do the drunk a favour by walking away from his advances.

My Capoeira beauty...

Dominic shook his head. It was unlikely that he would ever see her again. His bar was fairly successful. Different people came in and out of here on a daily and nightly basis. It was likely that she'd be just another one-timer. But that didn't stop Dominic's fantasies from going down a particularly dirty rabbit hole.

The woman had only stayed long enough to drink the glass of replacement wine Dominic had given her and to give her statement to the police officer he'd felt obligated to call. The volume of witnesses had ensured that it was a straightforward report and the police took the drunk away to dry out. Dominic had stayed away as she'd spoken to the officers to give her statement. But she still pulled his gaze. He'd sat on the stool that she'd previously occupied and discreetly watched her. He couldn't hear much of what she was saying to the officers, but one thing that came across very clearly was her name. Willow Blake.

Willow Blake... Willow.

Her first name seemed to be in such contrast to the viper tattoo that she sported on her upper left arm, but it was very much in keeping with the sensuality she oozed.

When she'd finished giving her statement, she left. But, as she did, she found him with her eyes as he still sat on her previous seat. A little smile played on her red lips. She nodded to him briefly and was gone. Then, Dominic Made spent the hours that followed fantasising about all the things he could have done with her red lips and supple body.

All Willow wanted tonight was a drink. She didn't want company. She just wanted a drink. Never mind that the bar called Bar Made was busy. It had a nice vibe and cute fish, so she'd thought that it was as good a place as any.

She needed that drink because she'd been having a really bad day. Strike that, week... month... months... *a whole goddamn year*... So, when the gross-smelling drunk man started chatting her up, she was none too pleased. She thought she'd done everything she could to get him to back off, but the state he was in seemed to make it impossible for him to get the message. Unfortunately, she'd been forced to employ actions she did not want to, but felt she had no other choice but to.

In the last few months of her tumultuous life, only two things stood out to her as even remotely good. One was the new Capoeira school she'd joined to get away from her last one, *Cordao de Ouro*. Well, not so much the school itself, per se, just a particular individual there and those who had taken his side. She was really liking her new school, *Jogo Arrepiado Capoeira*. The master was astute and friendly, and she was grateful that he'd allowed her to so easily transfer over. The two schools had a lot of history together, so it was an easy choice to transfer there. The capoeiristas at the new place also seemed nice, but Willow was weary of getting too close to any of them. Despite numerous invitations to hang out from Gabriela, who was the wife of Sean, the school's instructor, she'd always politely made an excuse to turn her down. Willow wasn't ready to get fully absorbed into the extracurricular activities of the school. She was still skittish after what had taken place at *Cordao de Ouro.* She was there for Capoeira... the sport, the game, the martial art, the spirituality. It had kept her sane and centred for the last eight of the thirty years of her life. She could live without many things, but Capoeira was not one of them.

The other good thing, if she could call it that, was the tall, grey-eyed Adonis at Bar Made who'd looked at her like she was cake. The bouncer on the other end of his walkie-talkie had called him 'Dom'.

Was that short for Dominic?

He'd also called him '*boss*'. Willow wondered if he was the boss of the bouncers or of Bar Made. The man was a tall drink of water and by the way she felt her nipples harden under his gaze as she spoke to the police officers tonight, her body was not immune. Still, she wasn't looking to get entangled with anyone, not anymore, not anytime soon. She'd learned her lesson about getting involved with men who were too hot for their own good.

OUTPLAYED

Yet, now lying in her warm bed, it was his eyes that she saw in her mind's eye as she drifted off to sleep. She then had one of the dirtiest dreams she'd had in a long time. It was a dream that starred no other than the grey-eyed Adonis himself.

CHAPTER 2

- queda de rin -

A week later, after yet another encounter with her dick of an ex, Willow realised she needed another drink. The Capoeira lesson she had just left did not give her the prolonged stress relief that she had so craved. Rick the Dick, as she had taken to calling her ex, had pissed her off yet again with his unreasonable demands and she'd had enough. While she was in her Capoeira class, she felt fine. She'd played a few games in the *roda*, which was the circle the capoeiristas sparred in. She'd taken down two guys. She'd played the *berimbau*, the primary instrument in Capoeira, and she'd led the singing. She loved her new school. Yes, she had once again turned down Gabriela's invitation to hang out with a group of them, due to her weariness of socialising at a school, but the class itself was fantastic. However, as soon as she walked out the doors of the Sports Centre, the familiar fury washed over her once again.

No one had infuriated her in her life quite like her lying, cheating, douchebag of an ex, Ricardo Santos. Every time she saw his smug face, she wanted to throw heavy objects at him. But alas, she tried to steer clear of those baser instincts. So instead, she found herself standing outside of Bar Made for the second Friday night in a row, gazing at the cute fish.

I wonder if my Adonis is here tonight.

She had debated returning here, but it felt like some invisible force was pulling her back. She smiled at the bouncer as she walked past him and cautiously entered, scanning for her Adonis as well as any other overly inebriated patrons. She saw neither. Her heart sank but that was because her Greek God seemed to be missing in action. She walked over to the stunning fish tank she remembered from before as she contemplated her next move. The beautiful creatures swam around as if they didn't have a care in the world. Willow couldn't quite understand why she suddenly felt jealous of fish.

Screw this! I haven't come here just for him!

She told herself that she'd come here because she needed to relax with a cold glass of Sauvignon Blanc. She spun around and started to head to a free barstool. As she did, the door at the back of the bar opened and out walked her Adonis carrying two large wine boxes. His flexed biceps were toned, tanned and touchable. He put the boxes down and bent over to unpack them. He carried out his task facing the back of the bar as he loaded the items he'd brought out into a fridge.

Willow approached the bar and sat on the stool that was free between two couples. None of the other bar staff were free. So, raising her voice to a level above the din of the crowd and the soft background music, she spoke.

'Excuse me!'

Nothing. He carried on with his job.

'Hiya. Exc—'

At that moment, he came up to his full height and froze. Through the mirror in front of him, Willow could see shock reflected in his face. He slowly turned around and Willow's breath was sucked out of her lungs. With a devilish smirk on his face, he walked to her area of the bar.

'*Well, well, well*,' he drawled, 'if it isn't Lady Viper!'

Willow's lips curved into a smile. 'You remember me?'

'How could I forget?' he asked as he leaned on the bar in front of her. 'You brightened up an otherwise irritating week.'

Willow couldn't believe it, but Adonis was making her blush. Her cheeks were aflame under his gaze. 'Did I?'

'Oh, yes.' His voice was husky and his eyes didn't leave hers.

'How so,' she asked with a raised eyebrow.

'Let's just say, and pardon my French, but someone really pissed me off, so I was in a foul mood that night. Seeing you drop that guy... well, it kinda... *perked* me up a bit.'

Willow got the feeling that 'perked' was not the word he intended to say.

'Yeah... I wish I hadn't had to do that. Sorry if I disturbed your business.' She was sincere in her apology.

'No need to feel remorseful. The patrons haven't had a show that good around here in a long time, if ever.' The smile he gave her was rich and he showed his perfect, white teeth.

Willow couldn't help it. She dropped her head and giggled.

'So, what can I get you?' he asked.

She looked up to see that he hadn't moved from his casual lean on the bar.

'One glass of Sauvignon Blanc. Large.'

He raised his eyebrow but didn't say anything. He just nodded and went about retrieving a glass and the bottle. This gave Willow the perfect opportunity to observe him. The tight, black t-shirt he wore perfectly accentuated his physique. She was almost positive that he regularly worked out to maintain such form. His hair was cut low on the sides and the tips of the hair on the crown of his head were slightly grey to the darker brown beneath. Definitely, a dye-job, she thought, but a good one. His jaw was square and emphasised his perfect bone structure. He was at least six feet tall. The man was the complete package.

Just my type!

As he laid the now filled glass in front of her, she opened her purse to retrieve her card. He shook his head and held up a hand. 'On the house,' he said, as his eyes locked with hers again.

She smiled in thanks and then put her purse back into her handbag. When she took her first sip, the cold liquid didn't do what it usually did. It should have cooled her body down and quenched her thirst. But it didn't. His piercing grey eyes were keeping her temperature simmering near boiling point. She was so lost in thought that it took her a second to register that he was holding his right hand out to her.

'Dominic Made.'

Eventually, she followed suit. 'Willow Blake.'

His grip was firm, cool and it made her palm tingle. He held on to her hand for a few seconds longer than was normal, but she didn't mind prolonging the surge that travelled up her arm as he touched her.

'Made?' her eyebrow lifted in curiosity. 'Is that M-A-I-D, as in the domestic help, or M-A-D-E, like the bar's name?'

He chuckled. 'The latter.'

'Ah, I see what you did there. You have a sense of humour.' She chuckled.

'On occasion.'

Willow took a long sip of her wine and looked around the bar. It was a nice place, but that wasn't the reason she had a sudden need to find another place to focus her eyes.

'Nice place you have here, Dominic,' she said as she had no other choice but to bring her eyes back to his.

'Thank you, Willow. *I* like it.'

The look of amusement then left his face as he asked, 'Are you here *alone* again, Willow?'

His eyes bore into her, pinning her to the spot.

'Yes,' she said huskily. 'I'm here alone.'

'Why?' His casual tone belied his curiosity.

'Because I'm not in the mood for company.'

'*Ah*, I see... hint taken.' He shifted and went to move away from the bar, his face full of something like regret.

On impulse, she reached over and put her hand on his, before he could pull his away from the bar.

'I mean, I *wasn't*... in the mood.'

He glanced down at her hand that was touching his and then back up to her eyes. She saw him exhale the breath he was holding, and she smiled before slowly pulling her hand away.

He observed her for a few more seconds before he spoke. 'Would you mind if I joined you with a drink, Willow?'

Her smile widened. 'I would like that very much.' Willow saw a twinkle in his eyes before he nodded.

'There's a free table over there,' he said, as he indicated a lone table away from most of the others. 'I can be with you in about fifteen minutes if that's not too much to ask. There are some things I need to finish up in the back.'

'Sure. Take your time.' Just as she was about to get off her stool and head over to the table, she asked, 'I'm disturbing you from doing your job, aren't I?'

He smiled broadly, baring his perfect teeth again, 'I'm the one who asked you, remember? Go on, I'll be quick.'

⭐ Her heart pounded hard as she made her way over to the little table. A tea light in a small glass with a black lace pattern on it was placed in the centre. The light casted a shadow of the design onto the cream-coloured, marble-like tabletop. Though this table was partially secluded, she still had a clear enough view of the bar. Reminding herself to take slow, steady breaths, she sipped her wine as she waited for Adonis to join her.

What the actual fuck! She's here! She's actually here!

Willow's sudden appearance at Bar Made had thrown Dominic. He'd been fully resigned to never seeing the beauty again. So, when he heard her silky voice trying to get his attention and then made eye contact with her, he couldn't believe it. If he hadn't believed his lying eyes through the mirror, then turning around to see her in that navy-blue, V-neck top and stylish bob was all the proof he needed to know he wasn't dreaming. This woman had wreaked havoc in his dreams in the last week. Before she'd walked into his bar a week ago, he wouldn't have ever called himself a masochist. But there he was, night after night, indulging in fantasies of a woman he didn't know he'd ever see again. In fact, he was downright positive she'd never come back to his bar after having an altercation with that drunk. In his nightly dreams since meeting her, Willow had fulfilled every one of his sexual fantasies. On the flipside, he'd woken up in cold sweats, cursing her name because of all the torturous cold showers he'd had to take. But every morning, after he'd exhausted every expletive in his vernacular, he relived the pleasure of those dreams in his mind.

Now, here she was again, in the flesh, that sexy chocolate flesh, which glowed in the ambient light of the bar. He'd let her walk out of here once, having had no real one-on-one engagement. There was no way in hell he was going to let that happen a second time. His desire to take warm instead of cold showers in the morning depended on it.

⭐

I'm nervous.

As the light of the little candle flickered, Willow admitted her feelings to herself. She was so nervous that she had to take slow breaths to get herself under control. Taking sip after sip of her wine didn't help. The only thing that did help, at least a little, was when she saw him finally come back out of the room behind the bar. She watched as he said something to one of his barmen, then bent down under the bar to retrieve a bottle. He poured some into a glass, then he got another wine glass and poured what she was sure was another Sauvignon Blanc for her.

My, my... Aren't you thoughtful?

Just as he put the wine bottle back where it belonged, Willow saw the barman say something to Dominic, who then shook his head with a conspiratorial grin.

Boys... They never quite grow up...

OUTPLAYED

Dominic wound his way around the other patrons as he made his way over to where she sat. As he did, she could feel her cheeks beginning to warm up.

What a sight to behold!

'Sorry, I was a little longer than I said I would be,' he told her as he eased his big frame into the seat across from her.

'Not a problem. I just feel bad for the rest of your staff. I'm dragging you away from your job,' she said as she laughed a little nervously.

He shrugged. 'The place practically runs itself. My guys and ladies can manage without me.' He leaned on the table, putting his weight on his elbows, which caused his biceps to flex. 'So... why weren't you in the mood for company tonight, Miss Willow Blake?' he asked. 'It is "*Miss*", right?' He looked at her left hand.

The smile he gave her then made her toes curl. 'Ah... yes, it is. As for the "why", let's just say, there are certain elements of my life right now which have got under my skin and really need to be excised.'

One of his eyebrows shot up. 'I see. Aren't we a pair! Both of us sitting on our own in a bar last Friday, wanting to be alone, because people had pissed us off.'

'That's one way to put it,' she said, shaking her head as an image of Rick the Dick once again came to her mind.

'Tell you what,' he said, 'how about for the rest of the night, neither of us talks or thinks about the demons we both need excised?'

'That's a deal!' she said, raising her wine glass to his. They clinked and each took a sip. 'So... how long have you had Bar Made?'

'Ten years.'

'Wow! I really like it. I was just walking past last time feeling like I needed a drink and spotted your fish tank. It's what made me come in. And, of course, I saw the name of the place and that was amusing.'

'And to think I almost didn't buy that thing. I guess now I owe the fish my gratitude,' he said with a chuckle. 'If it wasn't for them, I would never have had the opportunity to meet the stunning Willow Blake, the lady with the viper tattoo.' He smiled. 'Pun intended.'

Willow caught the joke and smiled. 'Are you this charming to all the girls, Mr. Made?'

'Only if they're as beautiful as you.'

'Wow!' Willow giggled. 'Do you have an off switch?'

'Why? I bet men tell you how beautiful you are all the time.'

'On occasion.'

It was true, Willow had received this compliment and others like it often enough. But somehow, coming from the fine-looking man sitting in front of her, and given all the awful shit she'd been put through lately, it really was like a pick-me-up. However, to calm her fluttering heart, she focused instead on the wine glass clutched between her palms as she drew gentle circles around the rim with her fingers.

'If you were mine, I'd tell you that every day,' he said.

Her head snapped up and she met his eyes. '*Yours*? What, have we been transported back to the 1800s?'

A saucy smile curved on his lips and his eyes filled with mischief. 'I know you know that's not what I meant, Willow. You know I meant—'

OUTPLAYED

'I *know* what you meant, Dominic. But I'm not sure I know what to say to it.'

'You don't have to say anything, Willow. I just wanted to make it clear, if you didn't know already, that I want to get to know you.'

'I see,' she said with bated breath.

'Would that be alright with you?'

'Y...yes. I think I'd like that.'

With the rate her heart was beating at, Willow thought that she would agree to anything he wanted right now.

'The first thing I want to know is, why the viper tattoo?'

She laughed softly. 'That's a question I get a lot. "Viper" is my nickname.'

'Why would anyone nickname a beautiful woman like you "Viper"?'

Willow could tell that this perplexed him. 'Actually, to be more precise, my nickname is *Víbora*. That's Portuguese for "Viper".'

Dominic eased himself back in his chair and his eyes glinted with amusement. Then, he lifted his glass to his lips and took a sip. Willow watched as his Adam's apple responded with its normal reflex action, but all it caused her to do was squeeze her thighs together tightly.

He doesn't even have to try, does he?

He put his glass down and smiled wryly. 'That doesn't quite answer my question, Willow.'

She smiled. 'No, I suppose it doesn't, does it?' She took a sip of her wine before she continued. 'Remember I told you I do Capoeira?'

'How could I forget? With the way you executed those kicks a week ago, I was positive that you were professionally trained.'

'Do you know much about it?'

'Not much, I suppose, apart from watching a few YouTube videos. I know it's from Brazil. From what I've seen, I respect the style, though it was never for me.'

She nodded. 'Well, it's a Capoeira tradition for the master to give each student a nickname. That's the one I was given eight years ago.'

Dominic's face lit up with humour. 'And he called you "*Viper*"?' He chuckled. 'Or rather... What was the other word?'

With her best Brazilian accent, Willow said, '*Víbora*.'

His voice became sultry as he said, 'I like the way you say that... *Víbora*.'

Needless to say, his accent was not as good as hers, but his tone shot electrical sparks through her and she shuddered, which he misinterpreted.

'Did I just butcher your nickname?' he asked with laughter.

She joined in. 'Not *too* bad.'

'Good.' He took another sip of his drink and continued. 'I'm curious. How are the nicknames chosen?'

'Well, it depends. It can he based on your looks, your personality or the way you play Capoeira.'

'"*Play*"?' His eyebrow rose.

'We consider Capoeira a martial art *and* a game, among other things. So, we never say "*fight*" or "*spar*", for example, when we challenge each other in class. We use the word "*play*".'

'And which one of those was the reason for your master's choice of your nickname?'

OUTPLAYED

She smiled cockily. 'The way I play.'

'You fight – I mean, *play*, like a dangerous, venomous snake?' He chuckled. 'This, I have to see!'

'Maybe you will one day.' Her smile faded a little as she said that.

'Why do I get the feeling that with you, there's a lot more than meets the eye?' He looked straight at her, tilting his head, as if he was searching her face for something.

'A little mystery is good for the soul, don't you think?'

'Yes... I do.' His stare grew more intense.

'So...' She was getting flustered. 'What do you like to do to blow off steam?'

His eyebrow raised and a naughty glint came to his eyes.

'Well, if that isn't a loaded question, I don't know what is.' He shook his head and smiled. 'I dabble in a few martial arts too.'

'*Really*? Which?'

'Jujitsu, Taekwondo and Krav Maga.'

'Wow! That's amazing! My Capoeira master also does Brazilian Jujitsu. How long have you been training in those?'

'Jujitsu, since I was a kid, and the other two for twelve and five years, respectively.'

'Nice! Those, I *would* like to see.' Willow couldn't help the sultry tone that came to her own voice.

Their eyes locked as they both took sips of their drinks. Then, she cleared her throat and asked him the first thing that popped into her mind. 'Are you from London?' It was the best that she could do to distract herself from the rapid beat of her heart.

He looked at her long and hard, as if he was debating with himself whether or not he would let her get away with her obvious distraction tactic.

Then, he seemed to relent. 'Cambridge, actually. I came to London to study at university and just never left. You?'

'I'm a Londoner through and through. I grew up in Whitechapel, but I'm in Shoreditch now.'

'Ah, an *East* Londoner. I like the vibe over there.'

'And what about you, Dominic? Where do you lay your hat?'

He smiled. 'Would you believe me if I told you that I live upstairs?'

She was just about to take a sip of her wine when her gaze flew up to his.

'Really?'

'Well, not directly above us, but on the third floor,' he clarified.

'Doesn't it get loud living around here?'

He chuckled. 'Well, I suppose maybe it does. But I'm used to it. Living in Central London is lively, never a dull moment around here. Isn't it noisy over in Shoreditch, the trendy and hipster capital of London?'

She laughed. 'You're right. I suppose it is.'

'I have to say, Willow, my new... *friend*,' he started, with a twinkle in his eyes, 'and I know I said I wouldn't bring it up, but I'd really love to thank the person who drove you in here last week.'

At his words, her stomach tightened. Some of how she felt must have shown on her face.

OUTPLAYED

'Sorry, I don't want to upset you, Willow, far from it. You walking in here last week was the one bright spark in my day. You just seemed to be... preoccupied, and not with anything good.'

'*My, my*, aren't you perceptive, Dominic.'

'Well, what can I say? I'm not just a pretty face,' he said with a wink.

'No, I don't think you are *just* a pretty face,' she added with a smile.

'You think I'm pretty, then?' he asked cheekily.

To that, she burst out laughing.

'*Yeah*, I suppose.'

'You *suppose*? You wound me, Willow Blake!' he said dramatically, placing his palms over his heart. 'You give a compliment and then so easily, you take it back?' He touched his forehead with the back of his hand and sighed like an overacting actor on a bad television drama. 'Was I wrong about you, Willow Blake?'

Fits of giggles rocketed through her body as she clasped her arms around her stomach, attempting to get herself under control again.

♣

As Dominic mimicked bad theatre, he relished watching her guard come down as she laughed without inhibition. He took in her beauty. The more he learned about her, the more fascinated he was by her.

He watched as her long arms encircled her stomach while she giggled. He took in how, what he assumed must be perfect tits, gently bounced as her belly-laughing continued. He knew he was perving on her, but he simply couldn't help it. There was just something about her...

'So, when you're not beating up drunks in bars, how do you occupy yourself, Willow?' he asked, attempting to refocus on something besides her physical attributes.

'I'm a... well, I *used* to be an executive at a financial firm. I managed a couple hundred people.'

'*Really*?' Dominic was impressed. 'And how long were you doing that?'

'Ah, about four years or so. Though, early on, I wanted to become a chef.'

'Is that right?'

'Yes. My father was an executive chef at a three-Michelin-star restaurant. Food is in my blood, I guess. I practically grew up in his kitchen. However, life took me down a different path, professionally.'

He could see the light in her eyes as she talked about food, but he also detected a tinge of bitterness as she spoke about the job she used to have.

'Did you enjoy your job, Willow?'

Her eyes flashed. 'Of course! I had a great staff who were excellent at what they did.'

He knew she was telling him the truth. But he couldn't shake the feeling that it wasn't the complete truth. He wanted to know more, but he didn't want to push her. He didn't want to scare her off and risk never seeing her again. He wanted to know everything about her, but he was a patient man. He could wait.

'It sounds like you loved your job. But you left...'

OUTPLAYED

'I did love it. We got such great work done. But I guess it wasn't meant to be.'

'So, what's stopping you from finding a new gig? A lady as talented as you should find it easy to get a new position.'

Her lips twisted to the side as she smiled. 'And how do you know that I'm talented?'

He smiled back at her. 'I can tell. I can see it in your eyes. I can see your drive and your determination. I can tell you don't do anything by halves. I like that in a woman.'

He studied her, noting the way she held her breath as he made those comments.

'You like that, do you?'

'*Yes*, I do.'

'I bet it would get old very quickly,' she said ruefully. 'I used to work pretty long hours.'

Something akin to sadness flitted across her face once again. She covered it up pretty quickly, but he was positive he saw it.

'If people are ambitious, they have to put the work in. There are no two ways about it,' he declared. He looked on as her breathing seemed to return to a normal pace.

'What about you?' she asked. 'You must have put a lot of work into this place over the years.'

He finished off the last of his drink before he went on.

'You could say that. There have been tough years. All businesses have those. But, like you, I worked my butt off, and here I am today.'

She smiled at him and looked down at her hands. To the untrained eye, it might have seemed like she was inspecting her hands for something particularly interesting, but he got the distinct impression it was just a defence mechanism. He got up and walked around the table to her. If she realised that he'd got up, she didn't show it. Her gaze was still firmly fixed on the invisible particles on her fingers.

'Will?' When she didn't look up, he placed his index finger beneath her chin and tilted her head up so that she had no choice but to look at him. What he saw was a multitude of emotions flying across her face, each flashing across her eyes in quick succession. It nearly took his breath away. With his index finger still in place, he raised his thumb up and gently brushed it over her lush bottom lip. Her mouth fell open and he saw her breasts rise as she took and held a breath.

His breath caught in his throat as he eyed her from this angle. She was a tall woman, but with her being seated and him standing, her height was null and void. He towered over her and for a little while, he forgot where they were, and he was able to completely block out the other people present in Bar Made.

'Willow?' To his own ears, his voice sounded raspy. With one last brush along her, what he now knew to be soft lips, he cleared his throat. Then, he brought his hands back to his sides. 'Would you like another drink?'

Still looking up at him, she answered, 'Uhm, maybe I should get going.'

Without thinking, he snapped out in panic, '*No!*' Something which he prayed wasn't fear entered her eyes. 'What I mean is,' he went on hurriedly, 'I would really like it if you stayed a little longer. I'm enjoying your company.'

He saw her face soften again.

'Well, I guess I could stay for a bit, but I'm going to need something to eat. I haven't yet had dinner.'

He felt a giant sense of relief. 'That, I can help you with. Do you like pizza?'

She nodded.

'There's a great pizza place a few doors down. They're open late. How about I buy you some dinner?'

'But don't you have to get back to work?' A flash of worry crossed her face.

He smiled. 'You see that tall guy serving on the right side of the bar?' he asked as he indicated. 'That's Jamal. He's basically my right-hand man around here. He can run this place better than I can with one hand tied behind his back. Everything will be fine. Besides, I'll let him know where he can find me if he needs me, which he won't. Trust me.'

He placed a reassuring arm on her shoulder and gently squeezed it.

'Come on, let's get you fed.'

★

As Willow sat in the booth at the pizza restaurant waiting for Dominic to come back from the men's room, she reflected on how the night had gone so far. The pizza dinner they'd shared was just what she needed and now she was just sipping on some cola. The conversation had flowed and he had her in stitches, just like at Bar Made.

She smiled to herself as Dominic's smiling face came to her mind. The man was a tall drink of water whom she was more than tempted to take a sip from. More than once, looking into his eyes had caused her breathing to go haywire. With great effort, she'd managed to get herself under control.

She was pleasantly surprised that in addition to being easy on the eyes, he also seemed to be incredibly intuitive, perhaps a little too intuitive a few times earlier in the evening. Willow wasn't a particularly closed-off person, but she liked her privacy. There were some things she had absolutely no intention of speaking about, to anyone, no matter how good-looking they were.

'Where did you go?'

Dominic's voice was a pleasant interruption into her reverie. She was so caught up in her thoughts that she hadn't noticed that he'd come back to the table.

'I was right here.'

'*Were* you?' He smiled. 'You seemed to be miles away.'

'Nope. Right here.'

'So, Miss Blake, are you tired of my company yet?' he asked as he lowered his large frame back into the booth, across from her.

'*Well*...' She watched as uncertainty crossed his face. She'd be lying if she said that it didn't please her to know that he didn't want her to leave. '*Nah*, you're okay, I guess,' she joked.

'Willow, you wound me again!'

'I get the feeling you can handle it.'

He chuckled. 'Well, Willow, as you can see, we're about to overstay our welcome here.'

Willow looked around the restaurant and saw that he was right. There was only one other table with customers and the staff were hovering nearby, clearly ready to close up.

'My guys and ladies at the bar have probably finished clearing up by now. You have two choices. You can have a final after-hours drink with me back at the bar or we can bring this party to a close and I can see you get home safely.' He smiled. 'It's your choice, although I know which one I would vote for.'

There was a twinkle in his eyes which she found irresistible. *Fuck it!*

With that thought firmly established in her mind, Willow smiled back at Dominic, got to her feet and said, 'Let's have that nightcap.'

CHAPTER 3

- bananeira - aú -

She said yes!

Dominic was bowled over. He had fully prepared himself to offer to give her a lift home on his Harley, or, if she didn't feel comfortable with that, offer her the number to a safe cab service. With his heart thudding, he paid the bill, got up, placed his palm on her lower back and led her out of the restaurant.

He let them into Bar Made with his keys as the bar was now closed. The main light was still on and Jamal was still there restocking the back of the bar for the next day's business.

'Hey boss. I wasn't sure I'd see you before I left,' Jamal said in his rich tone.

'Yeah, I'm glad I caught you. There's something I need to give you.'

Dominic turned and headed to the door at the back of the bar but then remembered his manners.

'By the way, this is my new friend Willow. Willow, this is Jamal, my right-hand man.'

OUTPLAYED

Jamal reached across the bar and extended his hand out to Willow, who was standing on the other side.

'Nice to meet you, Willow.'

'Likewise, Jamal.'

Jamal smiled conspiratorially, 'I remember you, Miss Karate Queen.'

That had all three of them breaking out into laughter. Dominic shook his head as he left them behind and headed to the back where his office was.

It was a small, but functional room. It had very few embellishments. Dominic always told himself that all he really needed in there was a desk, a lamp and the bar safe to secure the nightly takings. However, on more than one occasion, his sister, in her capacity as, well... *sister*, had overruled him and added some lighter touches, namely, a small, navy sofa, modern artwork and a well-stocked bookshelf. She had gone to great lengths to stock it with titles that she knew he would enjoy. There was just about everything from John Grisham and other authors in his genre. At the time, he'd complained that he wasn't here to spend his time reading. He'd said he would be far too busy with his customers. However, as time went on and the bar became more and more successful, he was able to delegate more to his staff, and his office had become like a bit of a sanctuary on a particularly strenuous day.

He picked up the white envelope that he'd left on his desk earlier in the evening and was back in the bar in under two minutes. When he got there, Jamal was getting into his jacket while still laughing with Willow.

'—dropping that guy was like seeing Michelle Yeoh in action,' Jamal said excitedly. 'That drunk was asking for it.

Though, if you hadn't done it, Dominic would've had to go Jean-Claude Van Damme on that guy himself.'

Willow's intrigued eyes found Dominic's.

'Don't listen to him,' Dominic said dryly. 'Jamal likes to exaggerate.'

Jamal rolled his eyes. 'Don't listen to *him*, Willow. He's entirely too modest. I've seen him throw down more than once.'

Willow looked at Dominic with amusement in her eyes and a smirk on her lips. He shook his head and handed the envelope he had to Jamal.

'I've finally finished that letter for you. I hope it helps.'

'Are you kidding me? This is sure to be the clincher. How could I not get it?'

Dominic caught the look of curiosity in Willow's eyes and apparently, so had Jamal.

'He's written me a letter of recommendation for my dream job.'

'You're leaving?' Willow asked.

'I hope so,' Jamal said matter-of-factly.

'Don't sound so excited about it!' Dominic said with mock outrage.

Willow and Jamal looked at each other and once again burst out laughing.

'You better get out of here before I take my letter back,' Dominic said with a chuckle.

'*Yeah, yeah*,' Jamal said, as he grabbed his backpack from behind the bar and headed for the front door. 'It was nice meeting you, Karate Queen.'

'And you, Jamal.'

OUTPLAYED

'You know she doesn't do Karate, right?' Dominic asked as he followed Jamal to the door.

'She told me, but *Capoeira Queen* just doesn't roll off the tongue in the same way, does it?'

Dominic shook his head. 'You're hopeless, Jamal. Now, get the hell out of here.'

'Bye, boss man,' Jamal said with one final flourish, and was gone.

Dominic locked the door and then opened up a small, locked box near the top of the door with his key. He pressed a button inside, which partially drew down the shutters. He then flipped a couple of the switches in the box which turned off the primary lights in the bar. The only ones he left on were the ones that illuminated the fish tank and a few of the small sconces dotted around the space, which he dimmed. When he turned around, he saw the look of anxiety that had taken over Willow's face.

'Are you alright, Willow?' he asked, concerned.

She nodded and he could see her trying to bring nonchalance into her expression.

'If you've changed your mind, it's okay. I can just take you home.'

After a beat, her face relaxed.

'No. I'm alright. *Really.*'

Dominic nodded.

'So, can a lady get a drink in this establishment, or do I have to go back there and ferment the grapes myself?' Mirth danced in her eyes.

He chuckled and started walking behind the bar. 'Coming right up, milady!'

Dominic went about pouring her another glass of Sauvignon Blanc and himself a bourbon. Then he came back around and sat next to her on a barstool.

He took a couple of sips and then turned to face her.

'I've had a really fun night hanging out with you, Willow. Unexpected, but fun.'

Willow glanced over at him with eyes that were full of mischief. 'Are you kicking me out, barkeep?'

'I wouldn't dream of it! I just wanted to make sure you knew that.'

She turned around and faced him fully, her fingers still clutched around her wine glass. Her chest was rapidly rising and falling. It was clearly a reflection of how fast her heart was beating.

'Willow...' To his own ears, his voice was breathy.

'Yes...'

So was hers.

'I hope I'm not overstepping in any way right now, but I'd like nothing better than to kiss you.'

He saw her sharp intake of breath as she asked, 'You'd like to what?'

He smiled at her. 'Willow, you are quite possibly one of the most beautiful women I've ever had the pleasure of meeting. With your permission, I'd like to kiss you.'

'*My*, *my*... aren't you polite...'

He started anxiously tapping his fingers on his leg.

'Well...' He pinned her in place with his hungry stare.

In lieu of answering him, she took a long swig of her wine, placed the glass on the bar and then got to her feet.

Dominic felt his groin tighten.

OUTPLAYED

Willow smirked at him wickedly and then walked over to the still-illuminated fish tank. It cast light and shadow on her face and her exposed arms, giving her skin an almost molten quality. This was one of the most mesmerising things imaginable to him. His heart quickened as he employed every ounce of self-control he could muster to stop himself from getting up off the stool and following her.

Willow didn't speak. She just stared at the tropical mix that glided through the water in front of her. She seemed totally absorbed by it. Dominic was astounded that two Friday nights in a row, he'd found himself jealous of the small, beautiful creatures that took up residence in the aquarium in his place of business. He shook his head and composed himself.

'Willow Blake, is it your intention to torture me?' Even though his voice had come out calm, he was anything but, on the inside. It felt like his heart was going into overdrive and he knew that there was only one thing that would quench this thirst that was comiing over him.

Dominic took a deep breath and forced himself to speak. 'Willow... would you like me to take you home? My Harley is just outside.'

She turned her head in his direction, then she shook it.

He exhaled... partially...

'Would you like me to call you a cab?' He held his breath.

She turned fully to him then and shook her head once more.

'Then, what do you want, Willow?' He couldn't help the tinge of desperation in his voice.

She didn't immediately answer him and Dominic, rather wryly, wondered if all of his held breaths in the last minute or so would begin to affect the oxygen supply to his brain.

'Will—'

'Well, are you just going to sit there and keep me waiting?' Her tone was suffused with amusement.

His brow wrinkled as it took a few seconds for the penny to drop.

'You mean...?' he trailed off.

'I mean, I would be more than happy to grant your request, kind sir!' She finished with an old-fashioned flourish and mock curtsy.

Dominic didn't need to be told twice. He was up from his seat in a flash. He stalked over to her, his groin doing figurative summersaults. He was with her in seconds and with his eyes trained on hers, he wound one of his arms around her waist and the fingers on his other hand found their way through her silky tresses.

He was too tightly wound to be gentle, so he crashed his lips down on hers. Her lips tasted oh-so-sweet, and then he took in the zest of the wine she had been drinking. His mind became overwhelmed with sensation as he continued to savour her.

He brushed his tongue along her lower lip and then suckled on it. He heard a whimper escape her and he smirked. His tongue danced around hers as a surge of need rocketed its way up his spine. He drew her in closer and enjoyed the way she moulded herself to him. His hand found its way down her back and then took in the perfect, pert curve of her backside. He was hard and he wanted her to know it, so he shifted himself slightly so that she got the full effect of his bulge. He pulled his head back from her a few inches so that he could make eye contact with her. She was panting and her eyes were ablaze. He wanted to give her ample time to make a choice about what she did or did not want to happen between them tonight.

'Will... you can feel how much I want you. But if you want me to stop now, I will.' He drew in a ragged breath. He was doing his best to hold himself together. 'So, should I stop?'

There was a wicked glint in her eye. 'No, Dominic. I do not want you to stop. Even if the building falls down around us, I don't want you to stop.'

He saw a pained look wash across her face before she did her best to try to mask it again.

Concern went through him. 'Are you sure, Willow?'

The next look that he saw on her face was that of irritation. 'For goodness' sake, Dominic! I don't want to talk. I don't want any more conversation. I just want you to show a girl a good time.' She smiled then. It was the same kind of smile she had for him when she'd first walked in here tonight. It helped him relax again.

'Ask and ye shall receive, my little viper.' He smirked.

She stepped back from him, took hold of the bottom of her top and then proceeded to lift it over her head.

Dominic's jaw nearly dropped to floor. Here she was, this little siren, practically half naked in Bar Made and he was lost for words and rooted to the spot.

'Will... you're... *beautiful*.' His voice was soaked in huskiness and need.

She dropped her top on the floor and then reached her arms around her back. He knew she was going for her bra clasp.

His eyes widened. 'Willow, stop! Please!' His tone was strong and commanding and she froze. He saw something almost like fear cross her face. Her arms came back around and meekly covered her exposed flesh.

'Please, I don't mean to alarm you.' He lifted his palms up to her in an attempt to calm her. 'Hold on a second,' he said quickly.

He walked away from her, hurried for the door that led to the back-of-house area and then made his way to his office. He was back with her in less than a minute.

When he entered the bar again, she was leaning her forehead against the fish tank. She looked stiff and she also clutched her top in her hand. He was almost scared to approach. He didn't want her to think that he was rejecting her, but he'd had no other choice but to command her to stop before.

'Willow, I'm sorry about. You see, I didn't want—'

'I get it, Dominic. You've changed your mind. You don't want to.' She cleared her throat. 'I understand.'

Confusion washed over him. 'What? You think that... Willow, *no*! Trust me, I *want* to! I want you so bad, it hurts.'

He heard her sharp intake of breath, but she still didn't turn around.

'Willow, here's the thing... The security cameras are on in here. If something is going to happen between us... I don't think it would be okay, for either of us, if I let them keep operating as normal right now.'

There was still no movement from her. In an attempt to prove to her that nothing had changed, he pulled his own t-shirt off, then walked closer to her until his front brushed her back. When his flesh made contact with hers, he inhaled sharply as electric shocks slicked through him. He reached down, took her top out of her tight grip and let it fall to the floor again. He stepped back a bit and drew his fingers up along her back until they settled on the clasp of her bra.

'Can I?' he rasped out.

She nodded.

He slowly undid both of the hooks of her bra as he took in a lungful of her intoxicating scent. He then drew the straps down her shoulder and let it fall too as he feathered light kisses down the side of her neck and along her shoulder. Without thinking, he surged forward, pushing her up against the glass of the aquarium as he nibbled on her neck. Her bare breasts splayed against it, giving the fish a show.

'Oh, cold!' she exclaimed.

'Dammit! Sorry,' he said. 'You've got my head in a spin, Willow. Where the hell did you come from?'

She chortled. 'Nowhere special.'

'I don't buy that for a second,' he said as he turned her around to face him. 'Exquisite!' His eyes drank in her perfect nipples. He lifted her up by her hips and she wrapped her legs around him. This time, when he pushed her up against the aquarium, she seemed to mind the cold less.

He went in and wrapped his mouth around her pert buds. He licked and laved his tongue along her areola. She tasted sweet and he already knew that he would not be able to get enough of her. He felt her fingers run through his hair and pull his head even closer. He continued to taste and pluck at her until she yelped out his name.

Without letting her go, he walked over to one of the long tables and put her down next to one of the short ends. He pushed away the candle centrepiece and then went to the buttons of her jeans. In no time, the zipper was down, the jeans were off and she stood before him in nothing but her cream-coloured undies.

Willow could barely contain the excitement bubbling up inside her. She needed this. From the first moment she met him, she knew that there was something about him, something that had piqued her interest. He was hot, without a shadow of a doubt. When he'd looked at her that first night, it was as if he couldn't keep his eyes off her. So, she'd come back, or was drawn back. And he seemed to be an okay guy. So here they were, and she needed this. She needed no strings and Dominic Made seemed to be willing to give her what she needed.

'Get on the table,' he said huskily.

She obeyed, fully willing to let him take charge. She'd spent too long taking on too much till she was at breaking point. There was nothing she could do about the rest of it, but this one time, this one night, she would let go and let Dominic…

She hopped on the table, perched on the edge and watched as he went to get his discarded t-shirt and spread it on the table behind her. His hands then went to his belt buckle. He undid it and his button, but he went no further on himself.

'Lie back,' he ordered.

Once again, she obeyed. He grasped her knees and gently pushed them apart.

'*Fuck me!* You're beautiful!'

OUTPLAYED

Before she could say anything, the breath was sucked out of her as Dominic pulled her panties aside and she felt his lips connect with her pussy. She opened her mouth, and nothing but hot air came out. His hot tongue laved its way up and down her folds, priming her for what was to come. Sparks flew through her body, igniting her innermost need. She was drenched and panting and out of her mind. Then his tongue eased its way inside her. She closed her eyes, gripped the edges of the table and placed her feet on his shoulders to anchor herself. He swirled his tongue around inside her and found just the right spot that drove her wild. He sucked on her clit as he also eased his long, beautiful finger inside her, adding to her building pleasure. He removed his tongue and she immediately felt the loss. However, it was only for a second though, because the next thing she knew, two of his fingers slipped into her and curved up. Her bundle of nerves reacted immediately.

'You're...so... *fucking perfect!*' Dominic rasped out.

Willow let out a moan as he began pumping her with his fingers.

'That's it, baby,' he growled.

Willow groaned long and deep as she started to wriggle around on the table. The sweet, familiar feeling started surging its way through her muscles. Just before she let go, she felt his lips go back to her folds.

'Dom!' she screamed out as she could control herself no longer. She also let out a stream of expletives that would make a pirate blush as her body went into spasms. Through her fog, she could feel him sucking up every drop of her juices and it made her come even harder.

Willow didn't know how long it took her to come back to the present. When her breathing eventually began to settle, she heard Dominic hustling out of his jeans and the sound of a foil wrapper. She found herself mesmerised by the dim lights that shone from the sconces around her. Her satiated mind had her feeling like the lights were dancing and—

'Ahhh...' Her breath caught again as she felt Dominic's tip caress her entrance. She looked over at him only to see the finest specimen of a man she'd ever seen in her life. The dim light of the bar reflected off of his glistening, sweat-covered torso. His muscles popped in all the right places. Suddenly, she couldn't keep her hands off of herself. She licked both of her thumbs, used them to lubricate her index fingers and then began rubbing her erect nipples between them.

'Dominic, please don't tease me,' she said as she looked into his wicked eyes.

He smirked and then with a swift thrust, he buried himself, balls-deep inside her. She screamed and twisted up her face.

'Fuck! Did I hurt you? Shit! I'm so fucking sorry, Willow. I lost control,' he said as he started to pull out, regret creasing his face.

'Don't... you... dare!' she commanded. She wrapped her legs around his fit arse and pulled him back towards her.

'But... you screamed, Will. The last thing I want to do is hurt you.'

'Yeah, I know I screamed. Just give a girl a second.' She smirked. 'You're a very... ah, gifted man.' His face relaxed then, so she went on, 'A girl has to have a little time to make room.' She winked at him and he broke out into a grin.

'Sorry. I knew that, but... I guess I got a little carried away,' he said bashfully.

Just before he pushed back in, she got a glimpse of his entire length and girth.

Mother of...

All thought left her as he slowly and deftly eased back inside her. He did it little by little, giving her the opportunity to acclimatise to him this time.

'Do—mi—nic...' He filled her completely. If she thought him going down on her made her feel good, then feeling every inch of Dominic Made inside her was like an out-of-body experience.

'Willow,' he rasped, 'you feel *so* good.'

His every thrust was slick. The smooth strokes had her eyes rolling back in her head. She felt like she was being possessed and that the only way she'd make it back to normal would be with a full-blown exorcism. Willow had had her share of sexual partners in her life. She had a healthy appetite and the men she'd been with had varied in their adeptness in the carnal arts. This man here, thrusting and eliciting grunts and groans from deep in her soul, was of a whole different calibre. Dominic was sexy as sin, hung like a god and an expert in giving pleasure. She'd come into this bar the first time looking for an escape from all the shit going on in her life, and this was turning into the best escape a woman on the run could ever ask for.

Dominic held on to her hips as he got even deeper. His muscles flexed with his every movement. When Willow refocused her eyes on him, she saw that his gaze was intent on her. Sensing the sweet build-up of the frenzy inside her, she started rubbing at her clit, and her hips began to buck of their own accord.

'I'm gonna come, Dominic,' she said through pants.

'*Come*, baby. I'm right there with you,' he said through strangled breaths.

When she could hold it no longer, Willow surrendered to the euphoria. Her body was awash with spasms. Soon enough, through her orgasm haze, she heard his beastly groan and felt his finger sink into the soft flesh of her hips. He stilled for a second, but a moment later, he let go with her name on his lips.

'Will...ow...'

He jerked repeatedly until with a final thrust, he'd emptied every drop of what he possessed inside her. His head and shoulders sagged and dipped. Without extricating himself, he fell on top of her, leaning his head on her shoulder.

⭐

'*Jesus, woman!* Where the hell did you come from?' he said, his voice a little muffled as his lips were on her skin. 'Having sex with a smoking hot, chocolate goddess, in my bar, is not what I had on my bingo card when I woke up this morning.'

She started to chuckle and he couldn't help but do the same. Unfortunately, there was an inevitability to this mirth. His penis decided that it'd had enough of its confines and slipped out of her.

Dominic lifted himself to his full height and quickly disposed of the condom in the bin.

'I must remember to take the rubbish out before my employees get here tomorrow. I don't want to give any of them a heart attack.'

OUTPLAYED

When he came back over to where he'd left her, she was now sitting up with her legs crossed and her still-pert breasts on glorious display. Dominic's eyes widened as he took her in again.

'That was... that was...' He didn't have the words to fully articulate what he was thinking.

She smiled. 'Yes, that was... something.'

He dipped his head and gave her a soft kiss on the lips. She responded in kind.

'What now, baby? My apartment is upstairs. Would you like to come up?' He eyed her intently.

'No, I can't. I've got to get home,' she said flatly.

He could not hide his disappointment. He would have liked nothing better than to whisk this woman upstairs to his bed and spend the rest of the night buried deep inside her. However, they'd only just met and he didn't want to push her. If he had to let her walk out the door now, he'd do it. But Dominic knew that Willow Blake was a woman he needed to know more about and her sweet pussy was something he would do anything to reacquaint himself with.

He cocked his head and said simply, 'Sure.'

'Can you pass me my bra and t-shirt?'

Dominic did as she asked, grabbing his own clothes in the process. She hopped off the table and started dressing. He followed suit, but for the entirety of the time they dressed themselves, neither of them took their eyes off each other.

Dominic watched as she went in search of her handbag. When she found it, she placed it on the bar and then turned to look at him. 'So, Willow Blake...' That sounded a bit too formal even to his ears. 'I met you for the first time, last Friday.

Then you dropped by again unexpectedly tonight. Will I have to wait another week to see if you decide you want to pop in again?'

She gave him a small smile. 'I don't know. I came back this week on impulse and because... well, I ah... thought maybe I wanted to see you again.'

Wow! She's honest! How refreshing.

Dominic didn't know many women who were willing to be this honest about what they wanted. In his personal experience, there were far too many who wanted to play games in order to get what they wanted.

'Obviously I'm happy that you dropped by. Can I have your number, Willow?' He didn't take his eyes off her for one second. He wanted to read her face to see what her true reaction to his request was. She gave nothing away.

'I... ah... I don't know if I'm going to come back here, Dominic.'

'And that's your choice, of course. You're clearly a woman who is not afraid to say what she wants and what she doesn't. And if you don't want to come back or you don't want to give me your number and I never see you again, it would be a shame... for me anyway. But I wouldn't hold it against you. But just in case, I'd like to contact you so I can know for sure and put my mind at ease.'

She smiled, reached into her handbag, took out her phone and handed it to him. 'Put your number in and I'll drop call you.'

He smirked and did as she asked. Then, he heard the familiar melody of his phone as she called him.

'So, you now have a couple of choices. I can order you an Uber or if you prefer, I can take you home. My bike is outside.'

'You ride?'

'Yes, I do. I have all my life.'

'Hm. I think I'm going to vote for the Uber.'

He laughed. 'What, are you scared of being on a motorcycle, Willow? Or just being on one with me?'

'Not at all. I like motorcycles.'

'So, you just don't want me to see where you live, then.' Dominic was amused by the discussion that they were having.

'Of course, I don't.' She smiled with mock coyness. 'I barely know you after all.'

'Do you always give men you barely know the best orgasm they've ever had in their lives?'

Her mouth dropped open and then she cracked up. 'You don't need to flatter me, Dominic. I'm a big girl. I don't need platitudes.'

He walked over to where she stood, grabbed her and pulled her into him, pressing his second erection of the night into her stomach. 'I don't play games, Willow. If I said it, know that I meant it. You're fucking gorgeous.'

With that, he crashed his lips down on hers and shoved her up against the bar in the process. He took bites of her bottom lip, forcing her to drop her head back. This gave him the perfect access to her beautiful, delectable neck. He trailed kisses down it and then licked the spots he'd kissed. She let out a groan and he knew that he had her under his spell once more. He felt her hand go under his t-shirt and caress his abdominal muscles. He took her lips again and then drove his tongue inside her mouth. She tasted delectable.

The next thing he knew, she'd opened the button on his jeans, pulled his zipper down and had her soft palms firmly around his dick, stroking him.

Fuck me! This woman is a vixen. No, scratch that, a viper... the Viper! And right now, even though she doesn't know it, she has her metaphorical fangs sunk so deeply into my libido that all I want to do is bend her over and fuck her senseless!

Before he could carry this out, she surprised him. She pulled away from his kiss and dropped to her knees, taking his jeans down with her. Then she grabbed his now engorged cock and wrapped her luscious lips around it. He gasped.

'Willow! What the...' he groaned gutturally.

He couldn't move. He was rooted to the spot. Back and forth, back and forth, her mouth went. Meanwhile, his brain went round and round, round and round.

This woman is going to be the end of me.

He looked down and watched in fascination as her head bobbed, ministering to his throbbing penis. She swirled her tongue around his tip and he gritted his teeth, trying to hold on to some semblance of self-control. It didn't work.

When she lifted his penis and ran her tongue along the base, he nearly lost it.

'Willow...*fu...ck...*'

She cupped his balls and continued her near assault on his senses. He was on the edge and he knew it.

'Wi...ll... I'm gonna blow any second.'

He watched as she cast her eyes up at him and winked.

The little minx!

She took her hands away from his base and instead grabbed his arse cheeks and yanked him further to her, his dick going deeper down her throat. When he hit the back, that was it for him. He didn't even have time to warn her. He shot out everything he had for a second time as his head fell back and his vision blurred. She released him from the confines of her mouth and panted. He tried to catch his breath, which came in jerky spurts.

'Sorry... Willow. I didn't mean to do that to you. I lost my head again... no pun intended.' He looked down at her, thinking that he would see a look of horror or disgust on her face. But he didn't. Instead, Willow was wiping off some of his cum from her cheek with her finger. She then proceeded to put that finger in her mouth and lick every last drop.

Fascinating! She's not a novice in this...

As soon as he thought that, he regretted it. The absolute last thing he wanted in his head was the image of Willow's hot lips around another fucker's cock.

'Wow!' he said. 'That was... *good*.'

Willow came up to her full height. 'Just "*good*"?'

'No, you're right. It was not just "*good*". It was *fucking fantastic!*'

'Now, I really do have to go,' she said turning away from him.

'But...' He was hoping he'd have more time with her.

'Sorry, Dominic. I really do have to. There's someplace important I need to be early in the morning and I want to be well rested and clear headed for that.' She pulled her phone out of her bag again and began tapping away at the screen.

Dominic, still standing there like an idiot with his pants down, felt a sinking feeling in his chest. He bent down to pull his boxers and jeans up, tucked himself in and then did up his button and belt. He ran his fingers through his hair in an attempt to calm his senses and stop himself from doing or saying something stupid... like begging her to stay.

'Alright,' he finally said. 'I'll call you an Uber.'

'Already done,' she said, turning and indicating her phone. 'It'll be here in seven minutes.'

Shit! That's all?

His chest tightened. 'Okay, so, can you just drop me a text when you get in?'

She glanced over at him with a curious look on her face. He could not read her. He had no idea what was going on in that pretty little head of hers. But suddenly, he felt like a sap in this little battle of wills. Willow held all the cards and brandished the better poker face.

She smiled. 'Sure, I will.'

She offered up nothing more of herself to him. And maybe that was for the best. He sensed that she was a woman who liked to keep her cards close to her chest. The absolute last thing he wanted was to make her think that he wanted more from her than she was willing to freely give. That was for the best for him too. His life was overflowing with complications at the moment, and some fucking fantastic sex like they'd had tonight was just what he needed. Theirs was an encounter he was sure he wouldn't forget till he was old and grey.

In the time he'd spent contemplating if he was ever to see this woman again, her taxi arrived and was honking outside. 'So, I guess this is goodbye then,' he said to her as his brow furrowed.

She slung her handbag over her shoulder and smiled at him wickedly. 'I guess it is.' She turned for the door.

OUTPLAYED

He snapped into action and walked over to the door to open the little box that had the shutter controls in it. He flipped the switch and the shutters started to move up. He then opened the door for her and they both walked out into the night air. It was warm, but he still felt the hairs on his arms rise. He put it down to dread he was feeling because he might never see this woman again.

He walked her to the car door, opened it for her and then blocked her from getting inside by standing in front of it. He gave her a sly smile. 'Willow, thank you for a… very memorable night.'

They both grinned. 'My pleasure, Mr. Made.' She went to get past him so she could get into the car, but he stopped her again by putting his arm out and pulling her to him once more. He tilted her chin up so that he could look straight down into her beautiful, brown eyes. He licked his lips and then dropped a soft, sensual kiss on her lips. She responded to him. He heard a soft groan come from her and that made him feel better. She may have been leaving, but he knew that this flame that had been lit between them, was not solely burning inside him now.

He stepped away from her and the open car door. She got in and then with one last smile, she shut it. His heart pounded as the engine started. He shook his head to clear away the giant, Willow-shaped fog that had lodged itself in there and the walked back into Bar Made.

CHAPTER 4

- martelo - negative -

The next morning, or rather, a few hours later, Willow slipped into office wear. She was not heading to a job. Of course not. It was a Saturday after all. It being Saturday wasn't the only reason she wasn't heading to a job while wearing office wear. The manner of her dress suited the occasion. She was wearing a dark-grey pencil skirt with a matching blazer and a white blouse. What she wore was perfect. It was plain, formal and had absolutely zero personality at all. It was the perfect outfit to wear to a lawyer's office to sign her divorce papers.

Why Ricardo had insisted on doing this on a Saturday morning was beyond her. However, she had acquiesced to his request. She no longer cared. She just wanted to be out of this sham of a marriage. In reality, the marriage had been over for a long while now. The legal end was just a formality at this point. She no longer wanted anything to do with the man. She wanted nothing else to do with his company, his money, nor his name. That's why, when she'd introduced herself to Dominic, she'd said her name was 'Blake', not 'Santos'. She didn't even want to think about it. She no longer wanted to be branded with the man's title.

OUTPLAYED

As soon as Dominic crossed her mind, she was transported back to last night. She'd showered and moisturized when she got home, but she swore she could still smell him on her. She could definitely still feel the imprint of where he'd touched her... where he'd buried himself inside her... She was quite sore actually... It'd been well over a year since she'd been with anyone, that is, other than her battery-operated boyfriend.

Long before they'd legally separated, Ricardo had stopped touching her. At first, she'd been devastated. She'd felt like she was a failure for not being able to keep her marriage together, for not being able to give him what he wanted and insisted he needed. However, after the way everything had turned out, she was glad to see the back of him. After today, she hoped she'd never have the displeasure of having to set eyes on him again. *Their* friends were mostly *his*. The company was his too. She'd poured her blood, sweat and tears into it, and she could objectively say that it wouldn't be what it was today without her vision. The house was his also. She was grateful that she'd never sold her own home when they got married. She'd instead decided to rent it out. He'd never really objected, though they didn't need the money. He was very well off.

Due to her tenants still being under contract when she moved out of Ricardo's house a year ago, she'd ended up in rented accommodation for a while. She'd inherited her house from her parents after they passed. She finally moved back in five months ago. Willow didn't care which aspect of their marriage Ricardo Santos kept. In fact, at this point there was only thing that mattered to her from her life with him. And that was *Cordao de Ouro*, her old Capoeira school.

SHONEL JACKSON

That's where they'd met. They'd both been members of the same martial arts school before they started dating. He'd been a *contra-mestre* then, which was the level just before master. Then one day, he started showing some interest. He was cute and a nice guy, so she'd said 'yes' when he asked her out. Two years later and they were married in a small ceremony. Her parents had never really warmed to him. They thought he was a good man, but they always insisted that his spirit never really matched hers... whatever that meant. Her parents used to like talking in riddles.

By the time they got married, with the retirement of their school's previous master, Ricardo went from being *contra-mestre* to *mestre*. He became *Mestre Lesma*. With the new title, came prestige. He'd earned it. He was a phenomenal capoeirista. His prowess in the Capoeira arena had never been the source of any problems between them.

They'd had a good life together, or so she thought. But after a few years together, when he couldn't get what he wanted, he emotionally checked out of the relationship. He spent more and more time on business trips and when he was at home, he may as well not have been there at all.

Their final fight was the last straw. The awful things he'd said were unforgivable, and public. The entire Capoeira school heard everything. The next day, she packed up and moved out. No way was she going to let him or any other man speak to her like that. No man who loved her would ever speak to her that way... no matter what *she'd* done.

So here she was now, wearing her plain and formal business suit, standing in front of the lawyer's office looking up at the doors. She wanted nothing more than to get this over with, but a part of her, she realised, was in mourning for the life she thought she'd have by now. She'd wanted to be settled with a man who loved her and a couple of kids. She wanted—

Well, none of that mattered anymore. She'd already made some big changes since the separation and in the coming weeks, she knew she had to make some more. Namely, on all her legal documents, she wanted, no *needed*, to officially go back to 'Blake'.

Slowly, but surely, she made her way up the stairs, her legs feeling like lead. She felt like shit. Here she was, only thirty years old and she was about to have a divorce under her belt. Leaden legs in tow, she pushed open the door and made her way through the opulently decorated, spacious hallway. She'd been here before. The first time was a few days before her marriage. Ricardo had brought her down here to sign their pre-nuptial agreement. She had no issue signing the document. His parents were rich and were the ones who'd pushed for the document to be drawn up. She loved him and she knew that he loved her and that's all that had mattered to her. No silly formality of a pre-nup was going to dampen her joy. They'd wed and she would be living her dream.

During the years that she basked in her joy, she'd forgotten some of the stipulations of the pre-nup. She'd forgotten the one that was chief amongst the others, the one that, if not fulfilled, could cause her to lose everything, husband, home and financial security. That particular clause had indeed not been fulfilled, or at least, *she'd* been unable to fulfil it.

So, here she was in the foyer of Spectre & Co. Solicitors about to put this chapter of her life behind her once and for all.

The secretary announced her presence through the intercom and then escorted her through to the conference room.

Shoulders back and chin up, Willow stepped through the door the secretary held open and then closed behind her. Willow stopped in her tracks when she saw one attendee that she did not expect.

'Priscilla?' Willow said with venom, her shock evident in her voice.

The woman flinched, as if she'd been struck.

Nicholas Spectre sat at the head of the conference table. Willow's lawyer Timothy Daniels sat on one side, with Ricardo and Priscilla, side by side, opposite him.

What the hell is going on here?

Priscilla Chumley-Smythe had been one of their closest friends. Clearly, *she* was still close to him. They used to be part of one big happy Capoeira family. Now, that was just another thing Willow had lost. They'd all got along well and Willow had considered her a trusted confidant. But now, eying the woman's smug smile and overtly cosy demeanour with Ricardo, Willow once again felt like one of the biggest fools in the world.

'Ah, Mrs. Santos. Good morning. Just in time,' said Mr. Spectre as Willow made her way over to the chair next to her lawyer.

Willow ground her teeth when the lawyer said her married name. 'Good morning... everyone.' Her, 'everyone', was ground out and spoke volumes.

Willow locked eyes with Priscilla, shooting daggers at her. Under Willow's scrutiny, Priscilla had the good sense to at least appear to be ashamed and just the right amount of nervous.

OUTPLAYED

Willow's scornful looks to Priscilla continued for so long that she missed everything Mr. Spectre had said.

'Willow? Do you have any objections?' asked her lawyer.

When she heard her name, she snapped out of it. Turning her head to him, she asked, 'What did you say?'

'Mr. Santos would like to offer you this sum of money,' he said, indicating the sheet of paper that he'd pushed in front of her. 'Despite the fact that the terms of the pre-nuptial agreement do not require him to do so, he feels that your contributions to building his company warrant this figure.'

Willow picked up the paper and looked closely at it. What she saw made hot fire flash through her body. A seven-figure sum was highlighted in bold at the bottom of the page.

'So, this is the value of the years of my life that I've given to you?' Nothing but distaste coursed through her tone.

'Willow—' Ricardo began, only to be cut off by his lawyer, who put a halting hand on Ricardo's arm.

'Mrs. Santos, I must emphasise that my client is under no obligation to offer you *any* funds. He is choosing to do this out of the kindness of his h—'

'If you're about to say "heart", I'll ask you to spare me the platitudes. I'm not for sale and offering me five million pounds for everything I put into our marriage is an insult,' Willow said.

'Well, I'm not giving you anymore!' Ricardo said in a huff.

Willow went on, ignoring Ricardo completely, focusing only on his lawyer. 'I came into our marriage freely. I gave of myself freely. I poured my professional expertise into managing his company, and I dare say I was damn good at my job. I did all of this because I loved him and us. So, you see, five million can never repay me for what I've given. The only thing that would have done that is fidelity and love. Ricardo Santos here, we all know, offered me neither.' She flashed a dark looked at Priscilla again. 'There is nothing he has that I would ever want again.' She focused on Ricardo. 'Keep your guilt money, Rick. Or better yet, give it to Prissy here. It looks like her Botox touch-up is due and you might need to help a girl out.'

Priscilla's eyes widened in horror and she self-consciously touched her forehead, presumably the site of her last injection.

'Willow, that's uncalled for,' Ricardo admonished.

'Alright, alright,' said Mr. Spectre, attempting to reassert some kind of control over the proceedings. 'Mrs. Santos, for the record, am I to understand that you are refusing to accept my client's offer of five million pounds?'

Willow's lawyer jumped in. 'Willow, please think about this fully.'

'There's nothing to think about, Tim. I want *nothing* of him.'

'Understood,' affirmed Mr. Spectre. 'In that case, we will stick with the original pre-nuptial agreement that was drawn up.' Mr. Spectre then slid some papers over to Willow's lawyer. 'You should find that those are all in order.'

Mr. Daniels scanned through them once before he handed them to Willow, offering her the pen he took from the inside pocket of his suit. Willow took it and signed without even one hint of hesitation.

Taking the papers back, Mr. Daniels handed them to Mr. Spectre, who passed them to his client. Ricardo took them, picked up a pen and then stared at Willow. If she was still a naïve newlywed, she would have interpreted his look as that of a man who was remorseful and sincere. Those days were over and Willow no longer had any shits to give.

'Sign the damn papers, Rick! I have places to be,' snapped Willow.

With that, he shook his head and signed all the pages he was required to.

Mr. Spectre took the papers back from Ricardo and spoke again, 'Okay. I'll have my secretary send a copy of this over to—'

Without even letting the man finish, Willow pushed her chair back, unapologetically scraping it along the floor as she did. 'Are we done? As I said, I have places to be.'

Mr. Spectre nodded.

'Alright then.' She looked down at her lawyer. 'Tim, I'll be in touch.' With one last venomous glance at Ricardo and Priscilla, Willow sauntered out of the room, slamming the door in her wake.

Willow poured out of the lawyer's office and barely stopped herself from running to her car. When she shut herself inside, it was then that she fully exhaled. She stripped her blazer from her body and threw it into the back seat. Putting her foot on the gas, she knew there was only one place she could go that would relieve the tension emanating from her pores right now.

Thirty minutes of winding through London traffic and she parked a couple of minutes' walk from her new Capoeira school, *Jogo Arrepiado Capoeira*. Stuffing her purse into her gym bag, she locked her car and started walking. When she heard her WhatsApp text message notification tone, she pulled out her phone absently and glanced at the screen.

SHONEL JACKSON

Dominic: Hi Willow. As you didn't let me know that you got home okay last night, I'm hoping you didn't get kidnapped by the taxi driver. Though with your abilities, I don't think he'd stand a chance! ☺

⭐Willow smiled, remembering Dominic's handsome face and sexy-as-hell physique. As alluring as he was, Willow knew she was in no mood to play text tag right now. She zipped the phone back into her bag and kept walking. She knew she needed to work this off in the Capoeira *roda*. Only then would she be able to stop seeing red.

Dominic had been up for a few hours. He'd had a good breakfast, tidied his apartment and was now on his roof terrace doing his morning workout. He was wired and his senses were hyperactive. There was a zing of energy surging through his body, and he was under no illusions as to where these sensations were coming from. The culprit that had taken hold of him was a beautiful, tall, slim, brown woman who was mysterious as hell. She had a wicked tongue and a killer spinning kick.

He hadn't heard from her last night after she left him. He'd played it cool and decided to let it be last night. He resisted and resisted for as long as he could before he cracked and decided to text her. He didn't want to come on too strong, so he went for mirth in his phraseology. He'd purposely chosen to send his message via WhatsApp because he wanted to know when she'd read it. He saw that she'd viewed it soon after he sent it. He waited for the tell-tale three dots, which would tell him that she was in the middle of texting him back. But the dots never came. He kept the app open for fifteen minutes as he waited, but there was no point. It was like a gut punch. So, he resigned himself to never seeing her again. He told himself that it would just be one of those once in a lifetime nights that would be just that... once. This morning, his workout was more to him that just his daily, morning routine. He pushed his muscles to the limit so that he could eradicate the image of the martial arts queen that plagued him.

CHAPTER 5

- au trançado -

'Hey, Willow!' came the cheerful voice of Gabriela, as Willow entered the Capoeira studio in the Sports Centre. Willow liked her. Gabriela had been nice to her ever since she'd moved to this school four months ago. She'd invited Willow to the weekly nights out the school had, but Willow, still in her self-imposed stupor, had done her best to keep Gabriela and the other students at this school at arm's length. At her previous school, Willow was the life and soul of the party. She'd helped out her previous master in any way he needed. That is, until he'd cheated on her, and Willow could no longer stand to be around *Mestre Lesma* anymore. Ricardo Santos... her now ex-husband... her former Capoeira master... and now, a world-class arsehole. Who knew he would turn out to be as slippery as his Capoeira nickname suggested! '*Lesma*' translates from Portuguese to 'Snail' in English. *Mestre Lesma*... Master Snail... how apt, she thought. She'd lost her husband, her *mestre*, plus many of their friends who were at the school, as they'd taken his side in the breakup.

OUTPLAYED

Since she joined *Jogo Arrepiado Capoeira*, she'd been apprehensive about getting too close to the members of this school. It was likely a case of 'once bitten, twice...*freaked out*', and Willow didn't know how to pull herself out of the rut she was in, in this respect.

Willow gave Gabriela a brief smile and a tight wave as she entered and dropped her gym bag. When she arrived at the Sports Centre, she'd headed straight to the changing room to strip out of the remnants of her morning divorce. She was now clad in her all-white *abadas*, which was the Capoeira uniform. She blended in perfectly with all the other students in the room who were now in various stages of their stretches.

'How's everything with you, Willow?' asked Gabriela, who was now beside her.

'I'm good, thanks.' Willow hoped that she'd managed to mask the turmoil that was still going on in her mind. The way she felt right now, all she wanted to do was hit something. Since hitting her fellow students was frowned upon by the *mestre*, she thought opting for the *atabaque*, which is the African drum used to play the music while playing Capoeira, would do.

'I know you don't like hanging out with people from the school, but I thought I'd give it one last go and ask you again. If it's being around everyone all at once that's the problem, then maybe you and I could have a drink on our own. What do you think?' Gabriela asked earnestly.

Willow stared at Gabriela in shock. The other woman looked so hopeful that Willow felt a little ashamed of herself over how she must have come across to the other members of the school.

SHONEL JACKSON

They must think I'm stuck up and anti-social...

Willow asked tentatively, 'Is that what you think? You think I don't like the people here?'

Gabriela's eyes widened and she bit her lower lip as she seemed to search for the words she wanted to say. 'Well... no, not really. Well... I guess we just don't know you yet. We would never push anyone to spend time with us. As you're new, we just wanted to give you the *Jogo Arrepiado* treatment and make you feel welcome and comfortable here. We're a pretty close-knit group. Didn't your last group spend time together outside of class?'

Willow's breath caught in her throat. This question had cut her a little too close. 'Well, yes... but I... I'm a very private person.'

Gabriela smiled. There was no trace of anger on her face. 'Don't worry, Willow, I completely understand. I promise we won't pester you with invitations anymore. I'll catch you later.' Gabriela then went to turn and walk away.

Willow reached out her hand and touched Gabriela on her shoulder to stop her. She wasn't sure what made her stop the other woman, but there was a part of her that felt Gabriela's sincerity. 'Are you doing something today, after the lesson?'

Gabriela beamed. 'My husband, Sean, is on toddler duty, so I was going to go have something cold with some of the girls here. You know Oksana, Jennifer and Aitana?' she asked as she pointed them out in the room.

'Oh, yes. Ah...' Warning sirens blared in Willow's head.

'If you want, it could be just us?'

OUTPLAYED

Willow closed her eyes briefly, took a deep, cleansing breath and spoke. 'No, it's fine. I'll join you. *All* of you. I'd be happy to. And it's overdue.' Willow was going for decisive.

Gabriela smiled widely. 'Excellent! It'll be great! I promise.' She patted Willow on her shoulder and then headed back to where she'd been before.

Willow felt her heart speed up. She wasn't sure that this was a good idea, but she also knew that her self-imposed exile from humanity was not healthy. From her observations, Gabriela and the other girls seemed nice, so she resolved herself to just take everything one step at a time.

After their warmup, *Mestre Escorpião* divided the students into two groups, the more experienced and the less so. He worked with the seniors and *Instrutor Raposo*, who was Gabriela's husband, worked with the others. Willow knew that coming to class today would help her to excise the pent-up frustration she was feeling about the turn her life had taken.

Soon enough, it was time for the *roda*. This word meant 'circle' in English. The *roda* was where the group would form a circle, the musicians included. Then, two students at a time would spar, or as the Capoeira world called it, '*play*'. Students showed off their best moves against each other while the others sang, clapped and gave their energy to whomever was playing in the *roda*.

Willow's still simmering emotions, made her follow through with her original goal of commandeering the *atabaque*, the African drum. *Mestre* took the *berimbau*, the bow-like instrument, which was the most important one in the Capoeira world. Gabriela took up the *pandeiro*, which was the tambourine. Then, *Mestre Escorpião* began to sing his song, followed by the rest of the students, in the 'call and response' style.

Ô, meu mano
O que foi que tu viu lá?
Eu vi capoeira matando
Também vi maculelê, capoeira
É jogo praticado na terra de São Salvador, capoeira
É jogo praticado na terra de São Salvador

The song spoke of the danger, tradition and discipline of Capoeira, while the chorus emphasised that the game Capoeira was played in Salvador, Brazil.

Willow always thought that this game was the most freeing thing she'd ever experienced. When she played in the *roda*, she was no longer Willow Blake. She was *Víbora*, another cog in the machine... in the fluidity that was Capoeira. She was inextricably linked with its history and the great players that had long since passed. She felt a connection with *Besouro*, who was a mystical and legendary capoeirista, with *Mestre Bimba* and *Mestre Pastinha*, the men credited as the fathers of Capoeira.

Ever since her private life had taken a nosedive, it was the beautiful game which had kept her sane, kept her grounded. It helped her to come to terms with the new direction her life had taken. Feeling this bond with the game was her lifeline, and she didn't dare let go.

As *Mestre* sang and played the *berimbau*, she followed with the *atabaque*, easily keeping up with the rhythm and joining in with the chorus of the song. Every time her palm came into contact with the animal skin surface of the drum, she felt a little bit of what had been consuming her ebb away. And, as she took in the game the two students inside the *roda* were

OUTPLAYED

playing, she let herself be swept away by the flow of their kicks, the litheness of their acrobatics and the mesmerising looks that passed between them as they attempted to mislead each other about which move they would perform next.

After a couple of songs, Willow surrendered the *atabaque* to another student and then signalled her intent to enter the *roda* and play. As she did, she heard Gabriela take over the singing. It had become obvious to Willow from the first week she started at this new school why Gabriela's nickname was *Canora*. The woman was indeed a songstress.

> *Dona Maria do camboatá*
> *Ela chega na venda*
> *Ela manda botá*
> *Dona Maria do camboatá*
> *Ela chega na venda*
> *E dá salto mortal*
> *Dona Maria do camboatá*

This song was about a badarse capoeirista called Maria, who goes to a marketplace and starts to exercise her authority and dominance over the people there. When she doesn't get what she wants, she busts out her Capoeira moves. For some reason, as Willow entered the *roda* with an *aú*, which is a cartwheel, she felt that Gabriela was aiming that song specifically at her, and it gave her an extra pep in her proverbial step.

Willow played with a guy nicknamed *Vagalume*, or Firefly, who was a highly accomplished capoeirista whom Willow liked playing with. Their game went on for about three minutes, in which time they both attempted to outsmart each other with kicks, takedowns and *floreios*, meaning flowery movements. They ended their game with a customary hug.

Willow rejoined the circle to clap and sing, and she gave what she now realised was cleansed energy to the next two capoeiristas that had entered the *roda* to play.

Four hours. That's how long it took for Willow to get back to him. The monotonous bar inventory that he had to do today was the only thing that had kept the sultry Willow Blake off of Dominic's mind. When he had to leave the storage area in the back room of the bar and head out to the front to help one or other of his employees, he'd been bombarded with image after raunchy image of the wild sex that had taken place here mere hours ago. If he never saw her again, he'd probably be continually haunted by the image of naked Willow laying astride the table in the bar. He had a friend who always claimed to be a shaman. He wondered if he'd need to call her and have her come in and burn some sage or something.

He was ticking things off on his clipboard and counting high ball glasses when he heard the familiar tone of his message notification. Without picking up his phone, he glanced at the screen, which he'd propped up on a box of wine. A surge of excitement ran through his nether regions when the name 'Willow' flashed up on the illuminated screen. He smiled as the clipboard clattered to the floor. Grabbing the phone, he couldn't read her message fast enough.

> Willow: Hey Dom. Sorry it took me so long to get back to you. You'll be happy to hear that I survived the cab ride and no worse for wear. ☺

'"*Dom*", huh?' he muttered with a smile. It gave Dominic a thrill that she was still being so familiar with his name.

OUTPLAYED

Dominic: Hallelujah! She lives! I was beginning to think you ghosted me.

Dominic watched as the three dots started flashing, indicating that she was typing her reply. Then they stopped and started a few times at long intervals. He realised that she must be choosing her words wisely.

Willow: Not at all. I've just had a lot going on today.
Dominic: Fair enough. So, will I see you again?

He thought that he might as well cut to the chase. There was no point trying to play it cool. He wanted nothing more than to see the delectable Willow Blake again. However, when fifteen minutes went by without a reply, he texted her again.

Dominic: How about I take you out to dinner tonight?
Willow: I'm not sure if I can.
Dominic: You plan on eating tonight, right?
Willow: Well, yes.
Dominic: Then I'm your guy. Come on, Will. Let me feed you.

Dominic waited for the longest five minutes of his life.

Willow: Alright. I'm out at the moment, but I'll need to go home first to get changed. I can maybe meet you somewhere by about eight.

Dominic: Perfect! Come by the bar, and we'll go from here. Btw, wear jeans.

Willow: Lol. Fashion tips from Mr. Made. Sure. See you later!

Dominic: Haha! I'm looking forward to it. See you!

SHONEL JACKSON

⭐ Dominic put his phone down and retrieved his clipboard from the floor. Doing Bar Made's inventory had never been as interesting as it was for the rest of the time he spent doing it that day.

Despite her fears of spending time with anyone from her new Capoeira school and getting too close to them, Willow was glad that she'd decided to finally take Gabriela up on her invitation to have a drink with her and the girls at a bar just around the corner form the Sports Centre.

They were all such nice ladies and had not tried to pry too much into Willow's life and background or the reasons she'd left her former school. They mostly stuck to light-hearted topics, current affairs and the state of their love lives. Willow realised that Jennifer was the biggest character of the group, and she told a lot of stories about her risqué private life.

'We're so glad that you're hanging out with us,' said Oksana. 'You're a frigging amazing capoeirista! I loved the game you played today with *Vagalume*. I love that you can hold your own with the boys in the *roda*.'

Willow smiled, appreciating Oksana's compliment. 'Thanks, Oksana. I like playing with Charlie. He challenges me and he's sneaky as hell.'

'You know what, ladies?' asked Jennifer. 'What do you think about us talking to *Escorpião* and asking him if we can plan a women-only *roda*? We've got a great group of very skilled ladies in the group these days. There's a whole different vibe in the *roda* when it's just us playing together.'

'Oh, that's a great idea!' exclaimed Aitana, punctuated even more with her strong Spanish accent. 'The boys can be so aggressive sometimes, puffing up their chests.'

OUTPLAYED

All the ladies laughed because they all had firsthand experience with what she was talking about.

'What do you think, Gaby? Do you think *Mestre* will go for it? Maybe see what Sean thinks? If we get *Mestre's* second in command on side, then he can get *Mestre* to let us plan it,' said Jennifer.

'I love the idea,' Gabriela said with a wide smile on her face. 'I'm sure my husband will like the idea too. I'll check with him when I get home.'

'We could even invite other ladies from some other schools,' added Oksana.

'Yeah!' they all chorused.

That is, except for Willow. She liked the idea too, actually, but she couldn't help but feel a little bit of apprehension about getting involved in making future plans with the school members. She'd spent so much time trying to avoid any real personal interaction with them that it seemed old habits die hard.

'Did they ever do women-only *rodas* at your old school, Willow?' asked Gabriela.

'Yeah, once or twice a year. They were always a lot of fun. As you said, Jennifer, there's an entirely different vibe.'

'Yep,' Jennifer agreed. 'It's a lot more *jogo bonito*, for sure.'

Willow couldn't help but giggle at Jennifer's assessment of women's games being more beautiful compared to the men's.

'You're so right, Jen. Us ladies do play a lot more beautifully than the guys,' chimed in Oksana.

After that, Oksana started saying something about her boyfriend and instantaneously, it made Willow think about Dominic. Not that she was considering him as a candidate for future 'boyfriend hood', not at all. Shaking her head, Willow brushed away that particular line of thought. She then discreetly pulled out her phone and decided to finally return his earlier message. As they sent messages to each other back and forth, Willow couldn't help the warmth that started to flow through her. She tried not to be too rude and did her best to still stay engaged in the conversation. As a result, there were a few long pauses in texting him back.

Willow knew that she didn't know him very well at all, except in the biblical sense. However, what she'd learned about him so far had her smiling at his jokes in his messages. Then he asked her out tonight and her breath caught in her throat. She felt her nipples harden and for the first time today, she was grateful that she'd decided to wear a formal suit. It had a jacket, and she hadn't taken it off when she first arrived at the bar. It was a fitting shield for her current predicament.

Did she really want to see him again tonight? Did she really want to take the risk of getting close to another man so soon after her divorce? She'd been separated from Ricardo for a really long time before their legal divorce today. However, she'd felt divorced in every way that really mattered ever since the separation.

Smiling at something Gabriela was saying, she contemplated Dominic's request. She let her mind wander back to last night and once again appreciated her brown complexion, because anything else would have made her blush blatantly obvious.

He's not an arsehole. At least I don't think so. He's fucking hot, and he knows how to use his god given talents. And he made me feel so damn good. How can I say anything else but 'yes'? If nothing else, he's funny as hell and good company. Fuck it!

Decision made, Willow sent another message agreeing to go out with Dominic tonight. Soon after, she put her phone away, as she contemplated which of her jeans made her arse look its best.

CHAPTER 6

- role -

Dominic checked himself one more time in the long mirror in his bedroom. He'd put on dark jeans, a black t-shirt with a small AC/DC logo on the top left of it and his black leather jacket. He knew he wasn't a bad-looking guy, but his nerves at seeing Willow again tonight had him spending far more time than usual in front of the mirror.

A few minutes before eight, he left his apartment in the private lift, which took him to the ground floor into the room at the back of the bar. As he exited, his phone pinged. It was a message from Willow.

> Willow: Hey, sorry I'm running a little late. The girls kept me out later than I thought I'd be. Be there in twenty minutes.

Dominic smiled. Tightness had immediately entered his chest when he read her first couple of words but then dissipated as he'd continued. He let her know that it was alright and walked through to the front of the bar. Saturday night was busy as usual with happy patrons.

Dominic went behind the bar, fixed himself one finger of his personal stash of bourbon and found a free high table to perch at while he waited for Willow. As he sat, he glanced around his bar. His eyes fell on the fish tank and he smiled. He was sure that anyone looking at him would think that he had something very good on his mind. And they'd be absolutely right. He found Willow Blake intriguing and even a little bit of an enigma. He could tell that she kept a lot under her hat. That first night he saw her sitting there at the bar, with a troubled look on her face, he thought that something bad must truly be going on in her life. The look on her face had mirrored his own, but he got the impression that her problems were a lot darker and more painful than his.

He wondered if she would give him more of an insight into what made her tick on their date tonight. As he thought about it now, he was hard-pressed to think of better sex he'd had in his life. The woman had brought out something almost feral in him. He'd never imagined that he'd be ravishing a sexy woman in his bar on a table, but that's exactly what had happened. She'd fulfilled a fantasy that he never thought he had, but was damn glad had taken place. He took a sip of his bourbon to calm whatever the fluttering was in his stomach.

Willow Blake, where the hell did you come from?

Before his thoughts could run away again, he spotted Willow outside as she came around a corner. Her tight, dark-blue skinny jeans hugged her hips and accentuated her toned legs. Over her white top, which showed a little of her midriff, she wore a black jacket. A small, dark-brown, leather satchel bag, big enough for her phone and purse, completed her casual outfit. Dominic had seen many women dressed in the manner that Willow was in right now, but none of them had caused his cock to throb quite in the way it had started doing now. Her bob of dark hair swayed gently when she looked side to side as she crossed the street. Dominic downed the last of his drink and then stood up to push open the door for her. For a split second, as he stood at the open door, he saw what he could only interpret as a look of shock in her eyes. He also noticed her chest rise as she held her breath. Sparks flew between them as time seemed to stop.

He was the first one to snap out of the trance as he signalled for her to come in with a flick of his head. As she walked past him, he put a hand on her lower back to guide her to the high table he'd been sitting at before. He didn't let her sit down, however. Instead, he turned her towards him, put his finger under her chin and lifted her face up towards his. He wanted nothing more than to stick his tongue in her mouth right then and there and transport them both back to the night before. As that wasn't an option, he instead elected to lower his head towards her parted lips. At the last second, he moved his lips a little to the right and kissed her softly on the smooth flesh of her cheek. From that vantage point, he could take in a lungful of her citrusy perfume. It made him want to lean her head back and lick the pulsating line of her neck. But, of course, he didn't.

When he pulled away and met her eyes once more, he saw that she had pulled her lips over to once side, showing off a dimple, and lifted her eyebrow on the same side.

'What?' he asked, intrigued as to what her expression meant.

'Mr. Made, I know we only recently met, but I didn't take you for a shy one.'

He chuckled. 'Why do you think I'm shy?'

OUTPLAYED

'Neither of us wanted you to kiss me on my cheek, but you did it anyway.'

She pinned him to the spot with her raised eyebrow again. Then they both burst out laughing.

He cleared his throat. 'I just thought that it was best to err on the safe side.'

'What's that supposed to mean?' she asked.

'Willow, if I kissed you on the lips now, there is no way that we'd make it out of this building tonight. I live on the third floor remember?'

He watched as she sucked in a breath, and it amused him to no end.

'Wait here for a second. I'll be right back.' He went to turn away but stopped himself and turned back to her. 'You know what, Willow, I can't wait to give you the ride of your life tonight.'

Her mouth dropped open and, in his mind, he saw her drool.

One of her eyebrows raised. '*Really?*' she asked suggestively.

He smirked, 'On my motorcycle, Willow. Get your mind out of the gutter.'

She chuckled. 'You should join me. It's so much fun down here.'

'I just might take you up on that. But let me feed you first. Be back in a sec.'

He turned and headed for the door that led to the back room of the bar and then into his office where he kept his motorcycle helmets.

Willow hadn't been on a motorcycle in a long time. In fact, the last time was when she was back in university. Her boyfriend at the time had a moped and he'd take her around a lot. He even let her ride it herself a few times. She wasn't great at it, but she'd always enjoyed being on it, whether on the front or the back. Somehow, she didn't think Dominic's bike would be as puny as her ex's moped.

A minute later, he walked back out from the back room with a smirk on his face and two black helmets.

'I thought maybe the lady would prefer an open face one instead of the full,' he said as he handed one of them to her.

'My, my, aren't you prepared!' She took it and shook her head. 'I guess you never know who might want to be taken for a ride.' Her tone was infused with more than a little snark.

He frowned. 'That one belongs to my sister. Sometimes she likes me to take her for a ride. She likes to be on motorcycles, though she hates riding them herself.'

Willow didn't know why, but hearing that the extra helmet belonged to his sister made her feel a lot better. She looked pointedly at him and just grinned.

'Come on. Let's get out of here,' he instructed, the smile back on his face.

She turned and let him lead her out the door and into the still quite bright, summer evening night. When he took her free hand, it sent a surge through her.

'My bike is parked around the corner.'

'What type is it again?' she asked curiously. She looked up at him as they eased through the Saturday night crowd. She saw the smirk on his face.

'Harley Davidson, of course.'

OUTPLAYED

The cockiness in his voice was self-evident, but she got the feeling he was only laying it on so thick for her amusement, not because he actually bought into some type of biker's bravado.

'Nice! I've never been on a Harley before.'

'Have you been on any bikes before?'

'My ex had a bike, but what he had pales in comparison to a Harley.'

He chuckled. 'Is that a recent ex?'

She heard a catch in his voice as he asked, and she got the feeling his curiosity wasn't as casual as he tried to make it out to be.

'Nah, he was from, like, a hundred years ago.'

'Ah.'

And that's all he said. She had a strong suspicion that his 'ah' was a lot more multifaceted than it appeared.

When they rounded the corner, she was confronted with a beast of a bike. It was black with red detailing on the fuel tank and the name 'Harley-Davidson' was emblazoned there. She didn't have the vocabulary to describe bikes of this nature, but it was definitely a head-turner.

She whistled in awe when she saw it. 'Is sexy a word people use to describe bikes? Because that's the only word coming to my mind right now.'

He grinned. 'You think my bike is sexy, do you? I can't say that I've ever been jealous of my bike before, but this may be that time.'

She rolled her eyes as they stopped in front of it. 'Dominic, I'm sure you're more than aware that you're quite easy on the eyes.'

'Are you saying you find me attractive, Willow?' he asked with a smirk and a raised eyebrow.

'With all the things I let you do to me last night, you bet your sweet arse I think you're sexy.' She winked. 'But you knew that already, didn't you?' she asked with her own smirk.

He laughed. It was a belly laugh which had her insides doing a weird little happy dance. His laugh lines made him look even more sexy, if that was even possible. Then, he hooked his helmet on his mirror and turned to her. Without breaking eye contact, he took her helmet out of her hands.

'May I?' he asked, but did not wait for an answer as he gently slipped the helmet onto her head. He then gathered the straps and secured it beneath her chin. With a sultry smile, he put on his own helmet, mounted the bike and flicked up the stand. Then, held his hand out to her and helped her onto the bike.

'Dominic, I just remembered. I didn't ask where you were taking me.'

He turned his head and she was treated to his equally sexy profile.

'No, I didn't.'

That's all he said.

'Well?'

'Well, what, Willow?'

She play-punched him in his kidney. 'Where are we going, smart arse?'

'You're just going to have to wait and see, won't you?'

With that, he started the bike and revved. Easing them out of the parking space, he slowly guided them into traffic. Willow wound her arms around him and settled in. Her memory of his body was as vivid as ever and she could feel every sinew of his muscles under his leather jacket. The man and his machine were as powerful as ever and right now, Willow was more than happy to be along for the ride.

⭐

Dominic couldn't lie. Having Willow on the back of his bike had him throbbing in all the right places. Feeling her pressed into him as he eased easily through Central London made him feel alert in a way he wasn't sure he'd experienced before. Playing it cool had never taken this much effort in his life.

Within twenty minutes, he exited the road into a parking lot and parked in a space at a supermarket. He put the bike on its stand and took his helmet off. She followed suit and then got off the bike.

'You surprise me Mr. Made. All that mystery for a trip to the supermarket in Camden Town? *Tut, tut, tut!*'

He took in the amusement in her eyes. 'Now, who's the smart arse? Willow, I promise it is not my intention to lay on my charm in the supermarket carpark. We just need to make a quick stop and then we'll be on our way. Our final destination is not far from here.'

Helmets in hand, they headed into the building. He guided her to the alcohol section.

'What kind of wine do you want?'

'Are you serious, right now?' she asked sceptically.

'As a heart attack.'

She chuckled and looked at the options on offer. Walking to the fridge instead of choosing one of the options on the red wine shelf, she took out a bottle of Sauvignon Blanc.

'I should have known,' he said.

'What kind of barman are you? I thought you guys had a great memory for your regulars' drinks,' she said with mock criticism.

'Ah, so you plan on being a regular, then?'

She smiled. 'We'll see.'

Holding back a laugh, he took the bottle out of her hand and walked towards the checkout. In no time at all, they were back on the road again with the bottle securely stored between them. A few minutes later, Dominic pulled off the road again. Bike locked and helmets in hand, he pointed to where they were going.

'Gua—Gana— How do you say that name?'

'Guanabana.'

'Gua... na... bana. Ah, Guanabana! What the hell does that mean?'

'It's a fruit.'

'I've never heard of that fruit before.'

'Some countries call it soursop. Maybe you know that name?'

'Ah, yes, I know it by that name. My mom used to love it.'

'This restaurant serves Caribbean and Latin American food. It's one of my favourites.'

When they were almost at the door, Willow grabbed his wrist to stop him. 'Isn't it against the rules to take in our own booze?'

He smiled. 'That's one of the beauties of this place. It's B.Y.O.B.'

'What does that mean?'

OUTPLAYED

'"*Bring your own bottle.*" They don't serve alcohol here, but for a small charge, you can, as the name suggests, bring your own bottle.'

She chuckled, 'I'm not sure if I'd call it a beauty, but you're the boss.'

He opened the door for her and followed her in. '*I'm* the boss, huh? You may come to regret saying that.'

He could see that she was ready with some kind of witty comeback, but the approaching host stopped her.

'Good evening. Welcome to Guanabana. Do you have a reservation?'

'Yes, under the name, Dominic Made.'

After checking his list, the host grabbed two menus and started towards their table. 'Right this way.'

Dominic hadn't been to Guanabana in a little while, but he could see that they'd done some redecorating. The walls in the front section had been painted white, while in the back, it was now lime green. The place was adorned with an eclectic mix of art depicting scenes and ornaments from the Caribbean and Latin America. Scattered about in various locations were wooden carvings from the African diaspora too.

Stopping at a table down at the back right next to the open patio door, the host asked, 'Will this table be alright for you? Or would you prefer to sit on the patio?'

Dominic looked at Willow and was happy to see that her face was beaming as she took in the atmosphere of the restaurant. 'Your choice.'

'Here's fine with me.'

'Have you joined us at Guanabana before?' the host asked.

'I've been here a few times,' Dominic said.

'I'm the newbie,' Willow said while raising her hand sheepishly.

'Well, I hope we're able to make you a regular too.' He placed the menus down on the table. 'I see you've brought a bottle of wine. Your waitress will bring you a bottle opener. Have a look at the drinks menu and see if you also want any of our soft drinks or mocktails too. The waitress will be over to take your order shortly.' He then excused himself and headed back to the front of the restaurant.

Along the two walls at the back of the restaurant were long benches with brightly coloured scatter cushions.

'Would you prefer the chair or the bench?'

'The bench, I think,' she said as she placed her helmet down at the end of the seat.

As she attempted to shrug out of her jacket, Dominic gave her a hand. When it was off, he saw that she was wearing a halter top. He'd never thought of shoulder blades as being a particularly sexy part of a woman's body, but surely Willow's exquisite ones would be in the top three of any shoulder blades competition.

He took off his own jacket and draped it on the back of his chair.

'Hand me your helmet,' she instructed. 'I'll put it with mine.'

Doing as she asked, he watched as she mounted hers on top of his. Then they sat down.

'Dominic, how did you find out about this place? It's so beautiful! It reminds me of some of the places my parents used to take me to when we went back home to the Bahamas. The artwork is gorgeous too.'

OUTPLAYED

He smiled. 'I'm glad you like it. I've been coming here for years. The first time was when a friend of mine booked it out for her birthday party. That was about... ah, maybe ten years ago. I've been coming and singing its praises ever since.'

'Ah! What's the food like? My family is Caribbean, so I have high standards.'

He held in his laugh... barely. 'High standards in all things?'

She eyed him suspiciously. 'Mr. Made, I do think you might be fishing.'

'What could have possibly given you that idea?'

She shook her head, refusing to take his bait. Instead, she picked up the menu.

'The food is excellent! I'm sure I've tried everything on the menu, unless they've changed some things since the last time I was here.' Dominic scanned the drinks. 'Hm, Guana Colada... I think I'll go with that.'

'What's that?'

'Mocktail.'

'Ah. You're not gonna have some of our wine?'

'I'm not much of a wine drinker.'

She chuckled. 'But you're into fruity mocktails?'

He shook his head. 'Well, when in Rome... I had a small bourbon while I was waiting for you at the bar. I don't want to have anything else as I'm the designated rider. Plus, I'll be carrying precious cargo. Gotta be on my best behaviour. I have some *high standards* I'm trying to keep.'

He winked at her and he watched as her chest began to rapidly rise and fall. Neither of them noticed that their waitress had walked over to the table.

She put wine glasses down on the table. 'Hello. Would you like any drinks off the menu?'

'Just one wine glass please,' he said. 'I'll have a Guana Colada and a bottle of water.'

'Sure, no problem,' the waitress said and she opened their bottle of wine. 'I'll be back in a few minutes to take your food order.'

'Thanks,' said Dominic.

With a little advice from him, Willow decided to order the Oxtail Butter Bean Stew, while he chose the Half Jerk Chicken. Both of their dishes came with Peas and Rice, and Plantain. They also had some Jerk Prawns to start.

After the food arrived, there wasn't much talking happening while they ate. Like many of the other patrons around them, all that came from their table was moans of pleasure and slapping of tongues.

'*Dominic! My God!* The food is *de-lish*! What the hell have they put in it. It tastes like it came from my grandmother's kitchen.'

He smiled. 'Well, I'm glad I brought you to a place with grandmother-worthy cuisine.'

'You sure did,' she said as she tucked into the last of her Oxtail. 'I'm stuffed! I think I'll weigh down your bike after this.'

'Hardly. If you want, we can walk off dinner by the canal?'

'Yes, please. It's been a while since I've come to Camden. I've always liked it up here.'

Dominic asked for the bill and paid. When they stepped back out into the night air, it was still quite pleasant. They left the bike where it was parked and headed for the canal, which was only a few minutes away.

There were a few other couples and individuals with the same idea. They were still carrying their helmets, so Dominic took her free hand in his. He was surprised at how natural it felt for him to do so. Willow had objected neither time he'd done it, so it felt right.

'I love it here. The water is peaceful, even though Camden itself is so boisterous,' she said.

'It is. Camden is one of my favourite places too.'

They walked along in companionable silence for a while, taking in the tranquil waterway. They walked under bridges and they watched as barges glided smoothly through the water. Their strides mirrored each other's and Dominic was hard pressed to think of a time when he felt more at peace. This is why he hesitated to ask her what he wanted to ask her. Last night, when she'd returned to the bar, he got the feeling that the subject was off the table. He didn't blame her. She may have given him a night of the best sex he'd ever had, but that didn't mean that they weren't still more strangers than friends. Still, he wanted to know. He wanted to know her better. Both in and outside of the bedroom.

'Willow? Would you mind if I asked you something?' As soon as the question was out of his mouth, he felt her hand tense in his and her step faltered.

★

Dominic's question had caught her completely off guard. The Camden Lock Canal was one of the single most peaceful places in London. She'd been lulled by its magic, as well as that of the large, warm, strong hand of the man currently holding hers. His 'would you mind if I asked you something' in itself was not some kind of harbinger of doom. But when had anyone ever initiated a line of questioning like that, when what they were about to get into were topics concerning sunshine and rainbows? She was convinced that it was a big fat 'never'.

Nonetheless, she took a deep breath and said as casually as she could muster, 'Go ahead.'

'That first night we met, what brought you into the bar alone and with that look of barely leashed fury in your eyes?'

She wasn't surprised that this is where his curiosity took him. The question was, how much did she want to tell him? Decision made, she went for the CliffsNotes version. 'That would be my husband. He—'

'You're *married!*' Dominic cut her off abruptly. He stopped walking and yanked her around to face him.

Willow looked into his eyes and saw shock, disbelief and something akin to disgust there.

'*No!*'

His jaw was set and she could see that he had his own 'barely leashed fury' going on now.

'Dominic, I—am—not—*married!*' She took care to enunciate every word.

'But you said—'

'Yes, I know what I said. Sorry, I unintentionally buried the lede there.' She took a deep breath. 'You asked me what brought me there. The answer is, in that moment, my husband brought me there. Am I married right now? The answer is "*No*".' She could see that her words had done nothing to soften his expression. She pulled him toward a nearby bench, relieved him of the helmet he carried and placed both helmets down at one end.

'Please, can you sit with me, Dominic?' When they were both seated, she went into the whole sordid tale. 'I was married for five years. To all intents and purposes and in the eyes of all our friends, we had the perfect marriage. Hell, it was in my eyes too. Then, just over a year ago, I found out he was cheating with one of our good friends from my former Capoeira school. Everything went to hell. He tried to convince me that it was nothing. That it was a mistake. That it was just a fling. He begged me to forgive him. Begged me to do couples counselling. Like the fool that I was, I bought it. To save the life we'd built, I decided to give him another chance. We did all the steps. The counselling, the couples' retreat, the lecturing from his mother on 'live and let live'. The shit that woman had to say to me made me see all of what she'd sacrificed to stay the wife of her own cheating, bastard of a husband. She told me that sometimes men stray, that it was how they were built and that we as women had to see past these faults for the good of the household.'

Dominic's mouth gaped open. 'She told you that? Was she from the Stone Age or something?'

A small smile quirked Willow's lips. 'I often wondered that myself.' His comment gave her hope that perhaps he was a little calmer. 'His affair never really ended. He just became better at hiding it. Eight months ago, I moved out of my marital home and filed for legal separation and then later, for a divorce. That night, I was drinking alone because I knew that a week later, the life I'd built, the husband I'd loved, the company I'd helped to build and so much more, was going to officially come to an end. From the moment I found out what he'd done, I hadn't let him touch me... in an intimate way. I told him that I needed time, and he'd agreed. He told me to take all the time I needed and that it was important if we were going build back the trust between us again. Turns out, he'd just continued getting his rocks off elsewhere.'

Dominic took her hand. 'Shit, Willow! I'm so sorry you had to go through all of that.'

'Thank you,' she said with a resigned smile. 'I signed my divorce papers this morning in front of Ricardo, who is the now ex-husband in question, our lawyers and Priscilla, the ex-friend whom he'd never stopped sleeping with. Needless to say, it's been a long time since I've felt married.'

'Jeez! That's a lot!'

'Sorry that I didn't tell you last night that I was still *technically* married, even if only a few hours later, I wouldn't be.'

'It's alright, Willow, I get it. Your ex-husband sounds like a real piece of work.'

She gave him a half smile. It was the best she could muster. She'd really enjoyed their date, but this conversation had taken it out of her and had unfortunately taken her to a dark place. However, she didn't regret telling him. She was glad she had.

'Dominic, would you mind if we headed back? I'm kind of tired.'

His face creased in regret. 'Dammit! I'm sorry that I brought all of this up for you, especially after we had such a great evening. I hope I didn't ruin everything.'

'I promise you, you haven't. I'm glad you know. I haven't really talked about it with anyone that was on my side. It's nice.'

OUTPLAYED

'I'm glad I could be of service. And I *am* on your side. Always...'

They walked back to the bike with a much different vibe in the air. Willow found that the purge was just what she needed, even if she hadn't realised it before. She'd been keeping far too much of this to herself, and for too long.

She gave him directions to her home and got off the bike when he pulled up onto her driveway. Despite herself, she did feel a little awkward. When she asked him in for a nightcap in what she realised was a very stilted way, he'd kissed her on the cheek and asked for a rain check.

'How about this, you get a good night's sleep tonight and I can pick you up tomorrow afternoon and we can do something then?'

'Oh, I can't tomorrow. Some of the students from my Capoeira school are going to the park for a little sparring and I'm joining them.'

His brows quirked up. '*Really?* Now that I would like to see.'

She belly-laughed. 'Would you now?'

'I would, actually. I've seen you in action once, remember? I would pay good money to see you kick butt again.'

She chuckled. 'Well, if you want, we'll be in Hyde Park from two o'clock. You're more than welcome to come watch.'

Before he left, Dominic got off his bike, pulled her into him and devoured her lips. Willow felt like she would never get enough of the man. Aside from their great chemistry, she found that she also liked talking to him.

He secured her helmet on the back seat with a strap and Willow watched him ride away with excitement bubbling up inside her. She was relieved she hadn't scared him away with her confession. She was worried when he objected to coming in but was then relieved when he suggested meeting tomorrow instead. She cast her mind back to their dinner in that Guana... something place. She made a mental note to ask him to remind her of the name when she saw him tomorrow. Both the succulent food and her handsome date brought a smile to her face which she would swear hadn't disappeared from the moment she entered her house, till she drifted off to sleep an hour or so later.

⭐

Dominic's ride to his place was one where he was barely focused on the streets that whizzed by. He was an experienced rider, so his autopilot brain got him home in one piece. When she'd asked him to come in, everything in him wanted to say 'yes'. But the hesitation in her eyes as she asked made him reply to the contrary. She'd revealed a lot about herself to him tonight. He got the feeling that she was still processing all that she said to him, and he wanted to give her time to do so. He wanted to give her space too. His instinct was telling him that Willow Blake was more than worth all the time that he would give her.

CHAPTER 7

- ponteira -

The night Dominic first laid eyes on Willow, *before* he actually spotted her, he'd been in a really foul mood. He was sitting there boiling over in his own personal fury. Earlier that day, he'd got some unexpected and unwelcome news. The news involved his father. Dominic had never in his life received news from his father which he'd ever found comforting. When he was a kid, his parents were married, but he'd always felt like he lived in a single-parent household. The man was never around. Dominic didn't remember receiving birthday and Christmas presents from the man, nor was he present at any of his football or basketball tournaments. Malcolm Made was around, but yet he wasn't.

One day, when Dominic was old enough to take care of himself and help his older sister Joy take care of their mom, Malcolm magically appeared back in their lives, wanting to atone for all of his transgressions. To say Dominic was shocked would have been an understatement. Malcolm charmed his way back into the family's good graces, practically prostrating himself before them. Joy hadn't bought it. Dominic, to his detriment, wanted to give him a chance. Malcolm had talked about how he regretted being an absentee father and not making much of a monetary contribution to his children's upbringing. Then, Malcolm offered to give Dominic twenty thousand pounds towards setting up his bar to make up for what he'd done. He'd said that the money was from his savings and that he was giving it to Dominic free and clear. Now, lo and behold, years later, Malcolm was saying that the money was a loan from some nefarious character. Malcolm was claiming that he had to pay the money back and that Dominic had to help. His father said he'd already paid back some of it, but he still owed over ten grand. Bar Made was doing very well, but a lot of the profits were already invested elsewhere.

Dominic couldn't just go to his safe and pull out bags of cold, hard cash. He was at a loss about the whole situation. The one thing that kept him from losing his cool with his father's constant phone calls recently was meeting Willow. Her presence in his life of late was very welcome for more reasons than one.

He was looking forward to seeing *Víbora*, the martial arts queen, in action in a few hours. He'd spent years honing his own skills in Muay Thai, Jujitsu and Krav Maga because martial arts had always fascinated him. He enjoyed the discipline the art forms taught. He also liked that a biproduct of learning these skills was that they helped to sculpt his body and train his mind. Though he'd never considered adding Capoeira to his skill set, he did find this, as many people called it, 'dance fight' to be a worthy art form. He'd never seen a fighting style that incorporated music and song into its practice. He'd also never seen one where the basic stance was not a 'stance' at all.

OUTPLAYED

He'd noted once that the foundational 'stance' that capoeiristas seemed to come back to after a sequence of kicks, wasn't stillness. It was instead a rhythmic triangle of steps with a swaying torso and swinging arms. It was fascinating. It wasn't for him, but it was fascinating, nonetheless.

He paid some bills and jumped behind the bar for a bit to help out before he got ready to head to the park to watch Willow train. She'd said that the group would be right near the Lancaster Gate Tube Station entrance of Hyde Park and that all he needed to look for was a bunch of people dressed in bright, multi-coloured trousers. As he slowed and turned his bike into the gates of the park, that's exactly what he spotted. It was a group of about fifteen adults and a few young children. When he parked, he noticed a few pairs of eyes from the group turn towards him, including Willow's. She smiled and waved at him. After taking off his helmet, he returned the gesture. This caused some of the group members' heads to swing towards Willow, but he didn't think she noticed.

He dismounted, secured his helmet and locked his bike. As he walked closer to the group, he realised that some of the female members were looking at him with intense appreciation. Though he was flattered, he only had eyes for one person there – the tall, brown bombshell, dressed is hip-hugging, bright-blue trousers with yellow and white stripes down the sides. She also wore a bright yellow sports top which cut off only a few inches below her breasts, so her entire midriff was on display. The other ladies present were dressed in much the same way, in an array of colours and designs. The men wore normal t-shirts with their bright-coloured trousers.

SHONEL JACKSON

When he got closer, Willow broke away from the chattering group to greet him. Instead of the kiss he would have liked to give her, he opted for a hug. When he straightened up, he could tell she was glad that this was all he gave her too.

'Hey.' he said softly.

'You made it!'

'I wouldn't miss it for the world,' he said as he gave her a wink.

'Who's your friend, Willow?' asked an Asian girl, who'd walked over to them. She had long, dark hair pulled back into a ponytail.

'This is Dominic. Dominic, meet Jennifer.'

This, of course, drew a few of the other members of the group over to them.

'Hm, in the interest of saving time, maybe I should do this all at once. Everyone, this is my friend Dominic,' Willow introduced. 'Dominic, this is Gabriela, her husband Sean, Aitana, Oksana, Omar, Ragnar, Wen, Hiro and our master, *Escorpião*.' Willow only introduced the ones who were closest to them. 'Dominic is a martial artist too and he wanted to watch.'

'*Bem-vindo!* Welcome!' said the man whom Willow had introduced as the master.

With a nod, Dominic said, 'Thank you for allowing me to see you all spar.'

'*Play*,' Willow corrected.

'Ah, yes, "*play*".'

The group around him dispersed and went on with their stretches and chatter. A couple of children who looked to Dominic to be about six or seven years old kicked a football around. Also, there were a couple of toddlers playing with their LEGO sets.

'They seem nice,' Dominic muttered to Willow who was still standing beside him.

'They are. It took me a while to settle in, but I think I've found a new home here with these guys,' she said.

Dominic watched as two of the guys picked up two large things that looked like bows with a large, round, ball-like contraption attached to one end. One guy seemed to be instructing the other. They were holding the ball part against their stomachs and using a long, thin stick to hit the string on the bow. It produced a scratchy, metallic sound.

'What are those things called?' he asked, pointing over at the men.

'*Berimbaus*. It's the fundamental instrument in Capoeira. Most of them are handmade in Brazil. The bow part is traditionally made from the wood of *biriba* tree. It's a strong, bent wood strung up with a metal string which is taken from car tyres.' Willow pointed out other parts. 'That thing that looks like a ball comes from a *cabaça*. That's a fruit. They hollow it out like a pumpkin at Halloween and let the skin dry. It becomes a hard gourd shell with a circular cutout on one side. That's the part you see them periodically touching their stomachs with. There's the stick they're hitting the string with, a flat stone which they touch to the wire to create different tones, and finally, the *caxixi*. It's a mini, woven, closed basket filled with seeds. That's a percussion instrument.'

'That's a lot of moving parts. How do they manage to hold on to them all at once and make such an interesting sound with it?' he asked.

SHONEL JACKSON

'It takes many years to learn how to play the *berimbau* well, and to learn all of the basic rhythms. I'm pretty good, but I haven't yet mastered it by any means. It takes months to comfortably balance the bow part on your pinkie finger alone.'

'They balance that giant bow on their pinkie?' He was shocked.

'Yep! A foot or so from the bottom, there's a fabric string wrapped around the metal string and wood. That makes the metal string tauter and helps to produce a crisper sound when the *berimbau* is struck.'

'It must hurt to balance it there.'

She chuckled. 'Yes, it does. But after a while, we get used to it.'

'Capoeiristas are more hardcore that I realised,' he said with a laugh.

'We try,' she said, and winked at him.

Dominic watched as two of the ladies he'd been introduced to earlier went over to the men playing the *berimbaus*. One of them took over from the guy who was being taught and the other lady picked up a third *berimbau* from the ground.

'Three of them? Do they need that many?'

'Often groups play with just one *berimbau*, an African drum and a tambourine. But it's also standard to have three. Notice that the *cabaça*, the round thing attached to the three of them are different sizes. Each of them produces very different sounds. The large one with the deepest sound, the *gunga*, is the leader and its player can dictate how the game goes using that one and which rhythm is played. *Mestre Escorpião* will play that one. The *medio* has the middle pitch and supports the *gunga*. The smallest one, the *viola*, is higher pitched. This one plays a lot of variations, like a singer who is doing the melody in a song. I think it's the most difficult to learn to play well.'

'It's fascinating.'

'Yes, it is.' She smiled. 'I should finish my stretches before we get started,' she said as she lowered herself to the ground, opened her legs and extended them as far as they would go. With a straight back, she began lowering her torso, face first, to the ground.

'Are you some kind of contortionist or something?' he asked, his tone full of amusement and lust.

Her stretch position made it difficult for her to laugh, but the trembling in her frame made it clear that that was what she wanted to do.

When she came back up to a seated position, she said, 'Nah, just years of yoga and gymnastics.'

Dominic knew that a good warmup and stretch was fundamental for any sportsperson, but watching Willow bend, twist and contort her body in all sorts of directions was making him feel like a very dirty old man.

'Okay, guys, let's start the *roda*,' said the master.

The group quickly finished up whatever they were doing and then formed a circle with the three *berimbaus* and tambourine players too.

Willow jumped up. 'Come on. You can join in the clapping,' she said as she took his hand and pulled him to the *roda*.

'What? How will I know when to do that?' he asked, a little trepidation in his voice.

'Just follow along with everybody else. You'll pick it up in no time.'

'We'll see about that,' he said under his breath as he joined the circle.

The master struck the largest *berimbau* and all chattering stopped instantaneously. He continued strumming it while moving it back and forth from his stomach. The sound was warm and commanding, and Dominic felt like he was being drawn in. After a few more beats, the master opened his mouth and released rich, tonal lyrics to a song Dominic had no hope of understanding. Yet, there was something in his phrasing which made Dominic unable to take his eyes off the man.

O meu berimbau de ouro, minha mãe, eu deixei no Gantois
O meu berimbau de ouro, minha mãe, eu deixei no Gantois
É um gunga bem falante que dá gosto de tocar
Eu deixei com Menininha para ela abençoá
Amanhã as sete horas p'ra Bahia eu vou voltar
Vou buscar meu berimbau que deixei no Gantois, Ha! ha!
Eu viva meu mestre
Eh a capoeira, camará

The song went on and at certain points, the entire group joined in and sang the chorus. Their voices raised the hairs on Dominic's arms. They also started clapping on a very specific beat and Willow gently elbowed him in the ribs to encourage him to clap like she was doing.

A man and a woman moved to stand near the musicians and waited. Dominic watched the master nod at them and then the two entered the circle and started to spar... er... *play*, as Willow had said. It was fascinating. There were some similarities with the kicks he'd mastered in his own martial arts training, but the most interesting difference was that no one seemed to be blocking attacks. They were ducking out of the way or escaping, only to immediately come back at the other player with a counterattack.

Different pairs tagged in to have a game. Soon enough, Willow left his side and entered the circle to play against one of the girls who'd been playing the *berimbau*. Watching Willow play was one of the single most arousing experiences of his life. She moved with grace and agility. She executed some spinning kicks similar to ones from Muay Thai. Then she landed and dropped to the ground with fluidity and swiftly attacked her opponent with ground movements. He realised that a capoeirista was trained to attacked from any position. They could be low to the ground, standing on their feet or flying through the air.

Aside from the two players in the circle, the third player seemed to be the music. Dominic thought that having it there added an extra, inexplicable dynamic to the game. As he watched, sometimes Dominic felt that the *berimbaus* were almost talking to the players and guiding their movements. The change in tempo and tone had a visceral effect on him which he couldn't remember ever experiencing before.

After an hour or so of action, the master made the final strum of the *berimbau*. The circle broke up and everyone started spontaneously hugging each. They all seemed to be experiencing some kind of shared euphoria. Dominic made eye contact with Willow as she hugged one of the guys there. Her eyes were glittering and her face was beaded in sweat. She never looked more beautiful to him.

She came over to him, her exhilaration evident in her eyes. 'Hey, I hope you weren't too bored through all of that.'

'Are you kidding? That was amazing. All of it was. The music, the vibe, everyone's so hyped... I don't remember seeing reactions like that after one of my Jujitsu lessons.'

She laughed. 'There's nothing that makes me feel freer than a few games in the *roda*.'

'You know—' he began, but was cut off by Gabriela coming over to them.

'Hey, you two. I just had a great idea. My father is babysitting tonight, so Sean and I are kid-free. How about coming dancing tonight at my club? A bunch of the others just said "yes".'

'You have a club?' Willow asked.

'Yeah. It's a great spot... if I do say so myself.' She giggled. 'It's called *La Duquesa*.'

'*La Duquesa* is yours?' asked Dominic. 'I've been there. You're right. It's a great place.'

Gabriela turned and beamed at Dominic and then winked at Willow. 'Willow, I like him. You should bring him tonight.'

Dominic smiled and then looked innocently at Willow.

Willow opened her mouth and then closed it again. 'Tonight? I don't know if I can. I have to—'

'Come on, Willow,' Gabriela encouraged. 'You know you want to!'

Willow was no match for the earnest appeals in their eyes, so she relented. 'Fine! Let's go dance the night away.'

Gabriela lifted her hand to Dominic for a high five. Willow smiled wryly, shaking her head, and Dominic held back a grin. He was, under no circumstance, going to look a gift horse in the mouth.

OUTPLAYED

Willow told Dominic she'd meet him at the club. She arrived fashionably late in a burgundy halter minidress, five-inch stilettos and a small black clutch in hand. She took in how stunning *La Duquesa* was. The gold and black décor added a touch of class to the establishment. She noted the two-tiered set-up. Gabriela had said that they'd be in the V.I.P. section in the upper tier, so that's where she headed. Walking gingerly up the industrial-style stairs, she cast her eyes around for her group. She spotted Jennifer first at the last V.I.P. table on the level and headed there.

'Hey!' exclaimed Aitana as she got to the table.

'*Mamacita!* You look hot girl!' said Gabriela.

'Hubba, hubba!' said one of the guys in the group.

The girls all surrounded her and double-cheeked kisses passed between them.

'You guys look amazing too. Gabriela, I love your club. It's got a really good vibe.'

Gabriela cast an appreciative eye around the place. 'Thank you. It's my baby. Now that I'm trying to open another spot, I'm losing my mind a little, but *La Duquesa* keeps me sane.'

'You're opening another club?' Willow asked, curiously.

'No, a restaurant. Well, I'm trying to. There seems to be one hiccup after another. And now the guy I earmarked to manage the place just fell through... Well, I don't want to bore you with shop talk.'

This revelation made Willow even more keyed into what Gabriela was saying. 'You're looking for a new manager?'

'Yep! And the grand opening isn't that far away.' Gabriela sighed. 'Well, watch this space!'

Willow thought quickly. 'Gabriela, would it be okay if I called you tomorrow?'

That seemed to take Gabriela by surprise, but then she smiled broadly. 'Of course! Anytime. I'll give you my number later. But for now, I think there's a handsome man over there who would like a bit of your attention. What a dish!' Gabriela said with a wink.

Willow turned around and saw Dominic. Her mouth went dry. He stood there with the light of the club casting shadows on his face. His gaze moved up from her legs to linger on her centre, peruse her torso, gobble up her breasts and then meet her eyes, a wicked smirk on his face. He wore a dark shirt with the top couple of buttons opened to reveal just enough of his chest to make Willow want to fan herself.

He walked over to her and she felt everyone else present melt away. He encircled her waist and pulled her into him. Wordlessly, he lowered his head and gently touched his lips to hers. His tongue came out and began probing at her mouth, demanding entry. Right now, she felt that she would give him anything he wanted. She wound her arms around him to try to pull him even closer. He kissed and sucked and nibbled on her lips until she started feeling weak in the knees. Her heartbeat picked up even more speed when she felt him hardening. Then, suddenly, to her irritation, he yanked himself away from her. She was panting when her gaze met his.

'Willow...' he rasped.

'Dom...'

'Maybe we should save this for later, hm?' he said as he smiled darkly.

OUTPLAYED

'I think that would be a good idea,' Willow said, as she tried to rein in her breathing.

They both slowly turned and Dominic put his arm around her waist possessively. Their group were staring at them slack jawed.

Jennifer cleared her throat, 'Dominic, do you have a brother or a really close friend who looks exactly like you?'

Everyone burst out laughing.

'No, but people do say my *sister* is practically my twin.'

Jennifer screwed up her face. 'Nah, she wouldn't have the requisite body parts I'm after.'

Willow shook her head. The little bits she'd learned about Jennifer so far told her that the other woman was a little spitfire with a quick wit and sharp tongue. Willow was sure that as she got to know her better, she'd like her even more.

'How about some bubbly, guys?' Gabriela piped up. 'Momma's got the night off, and I intend to make the best of it.'

A waiter delivered some bottles of sparkling wine and poured a glass each for the nine members of their group. They all enjoyed light-hearted conversation and every now and then a few of them took to the dancefloor. A few of the singletons got asked to dance by other clubgoers. Through all of this, Dominic kept a loose arm around Willow's waist. She had no objections at all.

'Wanna dance?' he whispered into her ear.

She nodded.

He took her hand and led her across the floor and down the stairs to the dancefloor. Rihanna's *Wild Thoughts* came on as they stepped on the floor.

How apt, Willow thought.

SHONEL JACKSON

She was pleasantly surprised that Dominic could dance... *really* dance. The pop song with Latin vibes had him swinging his hips and spinning Willow all over the dancefloor. At one point, he turned her around and held her hips as he grinded to the rhythm on her arse. She was on fire and Rihanna's dulcet tones had nothing to do with it.

A slew of songs came on which encouraged wining, gyrating, dipping and on a couple of occasions, twerking. To say Willow was having the time of her life would be an understatement. For the second time today, she felt completely free. For so long she'd felt trapped, both legally and emotionally, by her marriage. Now the marriage was behind her, and here was this man who seemed to like and desire her. If she was honest with herself, it scared the living shit out of her. Her ex's lies and deceit had knocked her confidence and trust. She didn't know where to place Dominic within the realm of her life. After all, they'd only just met. But, so far, she liked what she saw, how she felt and how with just one look from him or lick of his tongue, she forgot her own name.

After a few more hours of drinks, dancing and giggling with her new friends, Willow and Dominic took their leave. Willow thought that their antics on the dancefloor may as well be called foreplay for how turned on she was as they stepped out of the club and jumped into the waiting cab.

'Where to?' the driver asked them.

They looked at each other, their eyes ablaze.

'Your place or mine?' he asked huskily.

'Mine.' She gave the driver her address and spent the rest of the drive trying not to scream as Dominic gently squeezed and flicked her nipples through her dress.

OUTPLAYED

It took far too long to get to her house for Willow's liking. The front door closed when she was pushed up against it by Dominic. When his tongue connected with her neck and he began sucking, both her clutch and keys dropped to the floor and were forgotten.

'Willow,' he rasped, 'this neck has been driving me wild all night. These lips, these breasts and your fucking pussy are all I've thought of all night.'

He lifted her up and she wound her legs around his waist.

'Bedroom!' he rasped.

This was a command she was more than willing to follow. She pointed towards the stairs and he took them two at a time. He carried her like she weighed nothing.

'First door.'

When they entered, Dominic placed her down on her king-sized bed. She stared at him as he slowly stripped every item of clothing from his beautiful body. When his boxers finally came off, Willow soaked her panties.

'Come,' he ordered again.

She got up off the bed and stood in front of him. He spun her around, unhooked the button at her nape and slid the zipper down at the bottom of her open-back dress, letting the fabric drop to the ground. The next to go were her bra and underwear. When she felt his tongue circle one of her ears, she let her head fall to the side. He brought his arms around her body and cupped her breast. She moaned as he massaged and flicked her nipples. At some point, he must have licked his own fingers because she felt his now moist fingers tantalise her nipples. One of his hands trailed down her stomach and inched ever so closely to her centre. Her breathing stopped as she anticipated what would come next. When one of his fingers touched her clit, she lost it.

'You're so wet for me, Will,' he ground out.

He circled her clit and she sucked in her breath. She groaned as he pushed a finger inside her and pumped. He then took that one out and put two in instead. She clamped around him as he massaged her. He curled his fingers up just right and that was when she knew she was close.

'Dom... I'm gonna come...'

The words were ripped from her as he thrust his fingers inside and she panted. He sped up his pumping and she tipped over. With one last gasp, a scream peeled from Willow's lips. She rode the wave until her body went limp. Then he lifted her up and placed her quivering body on the bed. She watched as he retrieved a condom from his wallet and sheathed himself. Just as she remembered, he was thick and big and she was dying to feel him inside her again.

He got on the bed, his eyes not leaving hers for a second. He pushed her knees apart and held his tip near her entrance. She licked her finger and used it to circle her nipple and squeeze the already pert peaks.

With a devilish look on his face, he pushed his entire length inside her. His eyes closed as he held himself there. He pulled almost all the way out and then thrust back in. She panted as he held her knees and used them to anchor himself while he pounded her.

'Will... you're so fucking beautiful... so wet... so sexy. I'm never going to get enough of you.'

With every thrust, Willow tightened around him. He used his fingers on her clit and circled round and round.

OUTPLAYED

'Do...minic... *fuck*... That feels so good. Yes... *yes*...'

He pulled out. 'Get on your knees.'

She didn't hesitate. She gasped as he entered her from behind. Every time he pounded into her, she moaned. The crack of his palm over her arse was all it took for her to be pushed over the edge again. She came again, her juices gushing all over him.

'That's right, baby. That's right... come for me again.'

After another smack to her neglected arse cheek, she felt him take hold of both of her hips. Three more thrusts were all that it took for her to hear his guttural grunt of release. He groaned over and over as he emptied himself inside her.

She turned her head as much as she could and she witnessed his eyes roll back into his head, the muscles in his arms tightened as he clenched his fists.

'*God dammit, Willow!*' he rasped. 'You've put some kind of a spell on me or something? If you have, I hope there's no cure.'

She giggled. That of course had the effect of making him slip out of her. He took the opportunity to get out of the bed and slip off the condom.

He pointed to a door. 'Is this the bathroom?'

She nodded as she turned over and collapsed on the bed. Her body was rippling with sensations. She smiled as she remembered him saying that he couldn't get enough of her. It made her feel good that he'd said that. But she also had sense enough to know that as he'd said the words in the throes of amazing sex, that's as far as she should take them to heart. Dominic was hot and he was even hotter in bed. That's all she wanted, a man who knew how to pleasure her and kept things light.

Dominic walked back into the room with a smirk on his face. She let her eyes roam all over his chiselled body, inch after glorious inch of him.

'Like what you see?' he asked, not an ounce of shyness at her perusal.

'Love it!'

He slid into the bed and threw the covers over them both. He pulled her to him and she snuggled into him. Neither of them said a word for a long while. All she heard was the intermingling sounds of both of their deep breathing.

'Willow?'

His voice was as sleepy as she felt.

'Hm?'

'You're hot!'

She cracked up. When she got herself under control again, she smiled. She draped her arm over his torso and snuggled in even more as her eyes fluttered.

'You too, Dom, you too.'

A few minutes later, they both fell asleep with smiles on their faces.

CHAPTER 8

- aú batido -

There are few things better than morning sex. After Dominic fucked her when they woke up and then again as they showered together, Willow realised that she was a huge fan of morning sex. Especially when she had it with Dominic Made. She had a double shower and the man made very good use of it as be got on his knees, hiked up her leg and sucked her pussy like it was manna from heaven. The man was ravenous and she was more than happy to offer her body up to him as tribute. She'd got dressed, made them breakfast and before he left her house, he'd stripped her naked again, bent her over the sofa in her living room and slammed himself into her all the way to the hilt. To say she wasn't fully sated by the time he jumped into a cab, would have been a dirty lie.

After another shower, Willow finally felt able to start her day. Not having a job had given her a tremendous amount of time to think about what she wanted to do with her life, professionally. She had a bunch of qualifications in business management, accounting and public relations. One thing that she was positive about was that she never wanted to ever work again in a large organisation with hundreds of direct reports. She'd spent years doing that, helping to build her ex-husband's company. In all that time, she'd thought of the company as hers too. It was theirs and they were building it together. However, after he'd betrayed her in the worst possible way, the thought of being in an environment like that again made her feel nauseated. Settling into the plush, cream sofa in her living room, she picked up her mobile phone and hoped this was a good time to make this particular phone call. After four rings, the call connected.

'Hi, good afternoon, Gabriela speaking.'

Willow took in a deep breath. 'Hey Gabriela. It's Willow... Willow from Capoeira.' Willow didn't know why she felt she needed to be so specific about who she was and why she was stumbling over her words, but when she looked down and saw her left hand shaking, it all made sense. They'd spent a little more time together over this past weekend, but after keeping herself at a distance from all the people at her new Capoeira school for the last four months, she realised that she didn't really know Gabriela that well... or vice versa, actually. It crossed her mind that she was probably wasting her time, but she pushed on.

'Willow!' Gabriela said brightly. 'I'm so glad you called.'

The other woman's tone took Willow by surprise. 'You are?'

'Of course! Last night was so much fun. And your guy was so cool.'

Willow's chest tightened at this. 'Well... he's not really *my* guy. We only met recently.'

OUTPLAYED

'*Really?* Wow! I could have sworn you two had been together for ages. Your chemistry is off the charts. That man barely took his eye off you last night, or his hands.' Gabriela giggled.

'Well... I... ah... don't really know about that.' Willow felt her cheeks burn. She didn't really want to talk about Dominic. 'Am I catching you at a bad time?'

If Gabriela caught on to Willow's awkward change of subject, it wasn't evident in her voice. 'No. It's perfect. I'm in my office at the club and I needed a break anyway. What's up? You said you wanted to talk to me.'

'Well, you see, when you told me last night about your new restaurant and the issue you're having, it got me thinking.'

'Oh? I'm intrigued.' Gabriela was clearly curious.

'Well, are you still looking for a replacement for your manager?'

'I am, yes.'

'Where can people apply?' Willow asked anxiously.

'Well, I've got a listing up on Indeed, Upwork and a few other places, but whom do you have in mind?'

Here goes nothing, Willow thought. 'Me.'

'You?'

'What I mean is, I want to apply. Can I send you my resume on Indeed?' With every word that came out of her bumbling mouth, Willow felt silly.

'Willow, you want to work for me?' She sounded shocked.

'Well, I want to *apply*. I don't know if you'll think I'm a suitable choice or anything, I just wanted to have the opportunity to apply and be considered.'

'You know what, Willow? I'd love for you to send me your resume. I'll text you my direct email and you can send it to me.'

'I don't want any special treatment. I can send it like everybody else on Indeed.'

'Don't worry about all of that. All the applications come to me anyway. If you've got some time this week, we can even set up an interview.'

Willow was taken aback. 'Wow! *Really?*'

'Sure, no worries at all. But I have to warn you, the grand opening is a couple of months away. So, if I was to take you on, you wouldn't really start till closer to that time.'

'That is not a problem at all. I'm between jobs at the moment and I've enjoyed the time off. I feel like I'm ready to jump back into the workforce now.'

'Perfect! Ah, Willow, I'm so glad you called me. And I'm even happier that you came out of your shell with us this weekend. Us Capoeira ladies have to stick together.'

Willow laughed. 'I think you may be right there.'

'Dammit!' Gabriela said suddenly. 'I'm going to have to go. I've got an incoming call from the builder at my restaurant. If the last few weeks are anything to go by, it's not going to be anything good. *You* might be the one who doesn't want anything to do with my restaurant.' She laughed.

Willow smiled. 'I doubt it. Thanks, Gabriela. Bye. Good luck.'

'Catch you later, Willow.' And then she was gone.

Willow put down her phone and grinned wider than she'd ever done in regard to her career. When she got up and headed to her kitchen, the grin threatened to shatter her cheeks.

OUTPLAYED

The stupid smile Dominic had on his face when he arrived home was still there hours later as he worked out on his roof terrace. The only thing he saw as he lifted his dumbbells was Willow's face. When his doorbell rang, the stupid smile still hadn't gone from his face. However, when he answered the intercom and heard the voice of his caller, that did it. His father's voice and consequently his presence seemed to have its own sort of superpower, as if he was the Darth Vader father-figure of Dominic's story. In an instant, Dominic's state of mind shifted as he pressed the buzzer to let Malcolm Made come through the entrance for his apartment that did not go through Bar Made. When he went downstairs from his roof terrace to the living room and opened the front door, Dominic was sure his face was unreadable.

'Hey, son,' said Malcolm cheerfully.

'Dad.' It was all he could manage as he stepped aside to let him enter. 'This is a surprise,' he said drily.

'What, can't a father drop by to see his only son?'

Dominic didn't buy this for a second. There was no way his father was here solely for a casual visit. 'Not if said father's name is Malcolm Made.' Dominic couldn't help his derisive tone.

Malcolm spun around and plastered a look of hurt on his face. 'You wound me, son.'

Dominic shook his head and turned towards the kitchen. He needed a distraction and the best he could think of right now was to offer some kind of hospitality. 'You want a cup of tea?'

'Sure. You have any Earl Grey?'

'No. I don't.'

'Alright. Good old English Breakfast will do.'

Dominic busied himself with making two cups of tea. After he slid his father a cup, he looked at him pointedly. 'Why are you doing here, Dad?'

'You don't like beating around the bush, do you son?'

Dominic raised one eyebrow but said nothing.

'Fine.' Malcolm took of sip of the hot tea as they stood around the breakfast bar. 'You able to get that money for me, son?'

'Dad, when you gave me that money, I was under the impression that it was mine, free and clear. You said you were trying to make up for your absences when I was kid. You begged me to take it, remember? I didn't want to. Remember that?'

'Yes, yes, I remember.' Malcolm had the decency to look regretful.

Dominic laughed sardonically. 'Five-year-old me would say "*no backsies*". But I'm a grown man now and I'm the one who was stupid enough to accept your *gift*. I guess I was thinking like a teenage boy who was still desperate for his father to show that he actually gave a damn,' Dominic spat out.

'Sorry, son. I didn't mean for this to happen. But these people are dangerous and they want their money back now. I had some money coming in, so I was able to pay some of it back. Some of my... ah... income streams have dried up, so I don't have a choice here.'

Dominic had no desire to hear any more. He was done, in more ways than one. 'As I told you before, I invested the money you gave me years ago into buying and making improvements to the bar. It's spent. But here's what I'm going to do. I have some personal stock which I invested in a while back. I'm not sure how much is in there now or if it's even enough. I'll have a look and liquidate it. I'll put it back into your account when I do.'

Malcolm's still-pretty-handsome face creased into a relieved smile. 'I knew you would come through, Dom.'

Dominic ground his teeth. 'What an interesting choice of words.'

'What?'

'About me coming though. You dangled the carrot in front of me of us being father and son again, by offering me the money. But this is the stick, isn't it Dad? Yet another Malcolm Made scheme. More fool me! Now, I've decided to be "through" in an entirely different way. I'm through with you and any more of your bullshit and schemes.'

'Now, son. Let's not be hasty. I know I've upset you with this, but there's no reason to take it so far.'

Dominic barely kept a leash on his temper. It would do him no good to kick the arse of the man who'd contributed 50 percent of his DNA. 'Dad, I have to get to work. You're going to have to leave.'

'But Dom—'

'Please, Dad, I can't do this anymore.' With his patience spent, Dominic headed for the door. 'I have things to do.' He waited at the open front door.

Malcolm had trailed behind him. It was clear that he wasn't going to argue anymore. 'Alright, son. I'll leave.' Without a backwards glance, Malcolm walked out and headed for the stairs.

Dominic closed the door and leaned his back against it. In all of his life, there was one thing he'd become an expert in. That was, sensing when his father was lying. The talent had failed him when he'd accepted the older man's money in the first place. That had probably been because he was thinking with the brain of his desperate teenage self with daddy issues. With his common sense back intact, he was sure without a shadow of a doubt that Malcolm made was lying about something. He had a few tells, and he had tripped every 'tell' alarm that Dominic had memorised throughout his life.

He shook his head and eased away from the door. It was time for a shower and work. He had a lot to do before the bar opened this evening.

⭐

Willow spent the rest of the week preparing for her interview with Gabriela. After she had sent her resume, Gabriela emailed to tell her they could have an interview on Friday morning. Willow eagerly accepted the date offered and had been freaking out all week. She scoured her entire wardrobe to find the perfect professional look. She had many good outfits, but she couldn't decide which one was the best. Even though her father had been an executive chef, she didn't personally have a restaurant management background, so she did as much research as she could. She desperately wanted to impress Gabriela professionally so she could have a fighting chance to get the job. Her life needed a restart and this job could be it.

She'd decided not to see Dominic this week. It wasn't that she didn't want to. She did, but she was determined not to prioritise a man again over her own best interests. Lesson learned there. He'd asked her out again, but she'd let her down gently, explaining about the interview. Though she was sorely tempted to meet up with him, this interview was where her head was at. Right now, nothing else mattered. At least, that's what she told herself every morning when she woke up and saw a cute text message from Dominic. She couldn't deny that she liked him, that she wanted him, but right now, she was giving more credence to the brain in her head than the one that had taken up residence between her legs.

On Friday morning, a full twenty minutes early, she stood outside *La Duquesa* clenching her fists. After much deep breathing, she was able to unclench again. She made a quick call to Gabriela to let her know she'd arrived and then one of her staff let her into the building. They led her over the dancefloor of the now empty club. She felt her cheeks warm up as she suddenly had a flashback of her and Dominic tearing up that very same dancefloor.

Brushing those distracting thoughts from her mind, she ascended the stairs to the V.I.P. level and then walked through another door which led up some employees-only stairs.

'When you get to the top of stairs, Gabriela's office is the first door on the right,' said the young man who'd let her into the building.

'Thank you,' Willow said.

She mounted the stairs one at a time. At the door, with one last deep breath, she knocked. She was taken aback when the door was pulled open and she was greeted by Gabriela's beaming face. Before she could say anything, Gabriela had yanked her inside and given her a tight hug. She then followed up by planting two kisses on Willow's cheeks. This wasn't the first interview she'd been to in her life. There'd been many. However, she'd never been greeted like this at any of them.

'I'm so happy you're here, Willow.'

'Hi, Gabriela. Thanks for giving me the opportunity.'

Gabriela frowned a little. 'Don't be so formal, Willow. We're just going to have a chat. Have a seat over there.' She indicated the sofa. 'Can I get you something to drink? Tea? Coffee? Water?'

Willow smiled. 'I'd love some coffee... black.'

'How've you been? You weren't in class this week, so I was wondering.'

'No, I couldn't come. I was trying to get prepared for this interview.'

'Really?' Gabriela giggled. 'Willow, don't worry so much. I've seen your resume. If anything, you're *over*qualified. You used to manage a large amount of people at a Fortune Global 500 company for Christ's sake!' She brought Willow the mug of coffee and placed it on a side table. Then she took a seat at the other end of the sofa. 'What's made you want to get into the restaurant business?'

Willow glanced around the office. At the other end was a large, very tidy desk. The walls were painted red and one wall was all glass. When she walked in, she'd seen that the view through the glass was of the club. She liked the space. It was very comfortable and feminine.

'*You* did, actually.'

Gabriela's brows raised. 'Oh? I did?'

Willow smiled. 'I'll be honest with you, Gabriela. I haven't thought about working in the food industry since I was a kid, but when you mentioned your issue with your previous manager, it piqued my interest. What I can also tell you about is the environment I never want to work in again. I worked hard to get where I was and I worked hard to stay there. Hard work is second nature to me. But that high-powered environment sucks you in and it can be to the detriment of your private life. For the last few months, I've been reassessing what I want to do with my professional life. And I realise I want to work with people who have passion for what they do and where people respect each other. I'm a bit of a foodie too, so when you mentioned your restaurant, inspiration took over.'

'Wow, I'm glad I played even a tiny part in helping you figure out where your next steps might lie. The person whom I originally hired for the job had ten years' experience in restaurant management. But I swear the man couldn't tell the difference between a crêpe and a croissant. He came highly recommended too, so I put aside my instincts and chose him. Then, at the eleventh hour, he said he can't take the job after all. At first, it was a huge blow. Then I started thinking that maybe I dodged a bullet.'

As Gabriela continued, Willow took sips of the delicious coffee.

'I want someone who knows food, can manage people, is organised, can handle the paperwork aspect and who I can trust to manage my new baby. I've been trying to get this off the ground for a long time now and I need to be able to be on the same wavelength as the person I put in charge.'

'I understand. There's nothing worse than working with people who don't have your back when the going gets tough.' This particular statement was delivered with just a little more gravitas than any other she'd made since she arrived.

'I'm glad we see eye to eye on this,' she said with a smile.

SHONEL JACKSON

'Gabriela?' Willow started tentatively. 'Of course, I have no direct experience in *restaurant* management, but as my father was an executive chef, I practically grew up in a kitchen. I promise you right here, whatever I don't know, I'll learn. I'm a quick study and I'm dedicated. I'll work harder for you than I've ever worked for anyone else.'

Gabriela smiled brightly. 'You know what, Willow, I do believe that you mean that,' she said as she leaned over and patted Willow's hand on the sofa. 'Okay, so what do you know about Cuban food?'

Willow's eyes widened. 'I love Cuban food! *Ropa vieja*, *picadillo*, *yuca con mojo*, love it! I am partial to *empanadas* every now and then too. Why? Are you trying to figure out what you want to get for lunch?'

Gabriela burst out laughing. 'Not exactly. Although I would kill for some *boliche* right now. My restaurant will specialise in Cuban food. My dad is Cuban.'

Willow frowned. 'Really? Oh my God! I feel silly. I feel like I should have known that.'

'No worries at all. On the positive side, you seem to know your Cuban food.'

'Yeah, my best friend from university is Cuban. We used to share an apartment and she liked to cook. I, of course, liked to eat.'

'You know what, Willow? I've learned more about you in the last week and a half than I had for the nearly five months since you joined *Jogo Arrepiado Capoeira*. The more I've learned, the more I like.'

Willow smiled. 'Thank you. I know I've been a little standoffish, but...' She wasn't sure what or how much she should say. 'I've been going through a lot over the last year. It made me... not so easy to get to know. It's why I left my last Capoeira school.' With a deep breath, Willow took the plunge. 'I was married. My ex-husband, Ricardo, is also *Mestre Lesma*, from my former school.'

Gabriela's eyes gaped. 'I've heard of him. I think Sean may have mentioned him before, but I've never met him.'

Willow nodded. 'It ended... *badly*. He was... well, not the man I thought he was. So, this is me moving on and reclaiming my life.'

Gabriela shifted closer to Willow, her face full of sympathy. 'It sounds like you've been through the wringer. For selfish reasons I'm glad that this has brought you here. You're fun and beautiful and if your resume is anything to go by, you're also smart as a whip in the professional arena.'

Willow was glad that she'd revealed a little more about herself to the other woman. She was also happy that even though she'd done her best to keep the people at her new Capoeira school at arm's length, Gabriela had persisted.

'I have an idea. I've got about a half an hour of work before I go get some lunch. Wanna come with me?'

Willow smiled. 'That sounds like a fantastic idea. I didn't have much breakfast, so I'm famished.'

By the time Willow got home after lunch, she felt like she was on top of the world. She thought that even if Gabriela didn't offer her the job, it would be alright. Regardless, it was nice to dip her toe back into the professional world.

SHONEL JACKSON

The high she was on had her feeling all kinds of carefree and drove her decision about how she wanted to spend her evening. That decision involved a little black dress and stilettos.

CHAPTER 9

- bensao - esquiva -

His father's visit earlier in the week was still grating on Dominic by Friday. He didn't like being lied to and there was no doubt in his mind that that's what had happened. To make everything worse, he couldn't see Willow all week. He'd texted her every morning and she'd responded, but the conversations hadn't gone much beyond this kind of contact. He'd invited her out again, but she said that she had a busy week. He had to admit that he missed hanging out with her.

To blow off some steam, he'd gone to a few Jujitsu classes. That's where he'd been tonight too. For him, there'd always been calmness in the art form. Allowing himself to focus totally on the grappling techniques and joint manipulation of one of his preferred martial arts, took his mind off of his issues. With his father's deceit and Willow seemingly playing hot and cold, Dominic needed all the calm he could get.

He parked his bike in its usual spot and started walking back to his apartment. He wasn't working tonight, so he'd intended to walk past the bar entrance and head for the private entrance to his apartment instead. He glanced through the windows of the bar as he pulled out his keys and stopped. Someone sitting at the bar caught his eye and immediately his chest tightened. She was sitting on the corner of the bar with her crossed legs sticking out. His eyes traced upwards from her feet, which were clad in black stilettos. Still ascending, his gaze traced up her legs that went on forever. He assessed her figure-hugging black dress, long neck and smooth jawline. A few minutes before, he was convinced that she was playing games with him. Now, he couldn't care less. He'd missed seeing her more than he wanted to admit to himself. To have her here again sitting there waiting for him, surprising him...

He didn't even remember opening the door to Bar Made or walking past all the patrons to get to her. Instead of calling out her name, he put his helmet down on the bar and sat on the stool that was at a ninety-degree angle to her. This was coincidentally the same seat he was sitting in the first night he saw her. From the moment he stood near her, her eyes were on his. Not a word passed between them as they stared at each other. It was more of a 'smirk-off'.

'Hey, boss. Can I get you your bourbon?' asked one of the bartenders.

He wrenched his eyes away from her to answer his staff. 'Thanks, Nikki. And you, Willow?'

Willow indicated her still full glass of white wine and shook her head.

'Be right back,' the bartender said, and walked away from them to get Dominic's personal bottle of bourbon from the cupboard behind the bar.

'So... fancy seeing you here,' he said with a raised eyebrow. 'I thought you'd be washing your hair or something tonight.'

'I did that last night,' she threw back.

'*Touché.*' He chuckled. 'What brings you here, Willow?'

'I thought I'd drop in to see a friend,' she said as she sipped on her wine.

'A *"friend"*? We're friends now, are we?'

'Who says I meant you?' she asked, the smirk returning to her face.

'You have me there,' he conceded.

The bartender deposited Dominic's glass of bourbon in front of him.

'Thanks.' He took a sip and then looked over at Willow again. She hadn't taken her eyes off of him and he saw the playfulness inside of them.

'Where are you coming from?' she asked.

'Jujitsu.'

'Really? Now *that* I would like to see.'

'Would you?'

'Yes, I would, actually. I've always been interested in how the other combat arts work compared Capoeira.'

'Maybe I'll give you a few tips,' he said suggestively.

She grinned. 'I'll hold you to that.'

He looked at her pointedly without saying anything for a while. 'Willow, what are you really doing here, dressed so... enticingly?'

She blushed and took a sip of her wine. He did the same with his drink.

'Well, I wanted to see you.'

'Willow, you've been making excuses all week. Then suddenly you show up here dressed like that! What kind of game are you playing here on yet another Friday night?' He couldn't help the hard note in his voice.

Her brows furrowed. 'This isn't a game for me, Dominic.'

'Isn't it?' He'd already opened the door to this particular argument, so he thought he might as well walk through. 'The first time we met was because you came here. Then, the next, you showed up again and we had a fucking fantastic night. We hung out for a bit and then you practically ghosted me this week. Then, like before, you appear out of nowhere like all is well with the world.' He observed her reaction to what he'd said. He could tell that she was taken aback.

She adjusted herself uncomfortably on her stool and looked away. 'Are you saying you don't want to see me?'

'No, Willow. That is not what I'm saying.' He downed the rest of his drink. 'I'm saying I'm not here to be strung along.'

She gasped. 'You think I'm stringing you along?'

'You tell me. Look Willow, if you're looking for someone to be your booty call, then I'm not interested.'

Her eyes bulged.

'I like you, Willow. I want us to be friends. Friends don't ghost friends and then turn up out of the blue. I get it, we only just met. You don't owe me anything. But a little respect wouldn't go amiss.'

Even though he meant every word he said, a part of him wished he could have said it in a better way. He hoped she didn't think he was being too harsh. While he was speaking, she'd bowed her head. When she raised it and looked at him, he felt his chest tighten.

'You're right, Dom. I'm sorry. I didn't mean for you to think that I was using you. I like you too. I've been through hell with my ex-husband and I'm not sure I'm in the right headspace for much where a man is concerned. I did have a great time with you last weekend.' She smiled. 'You're kind of fun to be around.'

He couldn't help but smile too. 'Is that right?'

'Yes, but you already know that.' She took another drink and continued with a more sober tone. 'Dominic? Would you like me to go? Please be honest with me. I promise I'll completely understand if you'd rather not hang out tonight.'

He frowned, and then without another word, he stood up and got as close as he could to her. He tilted her chin up so they could keep eye contact. 'You came here dressed like a fucking goddess and you think I could send you away?' He smirked. '*Never...*' he rasped as he lowered his head and claimed her lips. Her taste was just as he remembered. It was nearly a week since he'd been able to kiss her like this, but it felt like forever. He suckled her lips and tongue, and moaned as he felt her give herself over to him.

It took an almighty effort for him to pull himself back. When he did, he saw the hunger in her eyes. 'We'd better stop, I think. I don't want my patrons to get the wrong idea about what kind of establishment I'm running.'

She giggled. 'You may be right.'

'Have you had dinner yet?'

'Not yet.'

'Wanna come up? I can make us something to eat.'

'I'd like that.'

He picked up his helmet and she picked up her clutch bag, and they headed for the door that led to the back area of the bar. Once the lift took them to his apartment floor, he exhaled a breath which he was sure he'd been holding since the last time he saw her.

'*Nice*,' she said as she cast her eyes around his place.

It was undoubtedly very masculine with a dark-chocolate-coloured sofa and white walls with artistically edited photos of famous movie fight scenes.

'*Bloodsport*. Huh! A Van Damme fan, are you?'

'Ah, you know your classics,' he said as he turned around to see the image she was looking at.

She smiled and looked at the next one. 'Hmm.' She searched her memory. 'Bruce and Kareem... ah, yes, *Game of Death*. And this one,' she said as she pointed to a third, '*Fong Sai-Yuk*. Jet Li is one of my favourites.'

He looked at her, his face full of fascination. 'I see we're both martial arts junkies in more ways than one.'

She smiled. 'As kids, my cousins and I were martial arts fanatics. Any Hong Kong cinema film released with Jackie Chan, Bolo Yeung or Jet Li and we were right there. Don't even get me started on the *Shaolin Temple* series. Those were classics.'

He chuckled. 'Yes... they were.'

'Of course, there's also Michelle Yeoh, Donnie Yen, Michael Jai White, Keanu Reeves and Wesley Snipes. I like any of their martial arts movies too. The cherry on top is that Snipes trained in Capoeira too.'

'Well, well, aren't you a fountain of martial arts knowledge,' he said, clearly fascinated.

She laughed. 'Sorry,' she said sheepishly.

'No need to apologise. You may be the only person I know who might rival me in martial arts movie trivia.'

They both laughed.

'Can I get you something to drink?'

'You know what I like.' She winked.

'That, I do. One glass of Sauvignon Blanc coming up,' he said as he headed to his kitchen area to get it for her.

It was a large open-plan space so she could see him rooting through the cupboards and fridge.

'I thought you didn't like wine. How come you have it so handy in your fridge?' She knew she was fishing, but right now, she didn't care.

He chuckled. 'I decided to start keeping it up here last week just in case any new "*friends*" decided to drop by.'

'Ahh... lucky I dropped by then.' She grinned.

'Very lucky. Okay... for food, you've got two options, sea bass or rib-eye. I'll do some potatoes and salad on the side.'

She considered her options. 'I'll take the sea bass.'

Forty minutes later, there was some piping hot food served up for them both. She dug into her food with gusto. It was delicious and she wasn't afraid to show her appreciation for its scrumptiousness by making groans deep in her throat.

'Willow, would you mind not making sex noises, or I won't be able to finish my dinner.' He stopped cutting his steak and put his knife and fork down.

'It's not my fault you're such a good cook,' she shot back. 'It's just so damn juicy.'

'I'm glad you're enjoying it.' He shook his head with a smile and resumed eating.

'Are you kidding? This is the best sea bass I've ever tasted. Who taught you to cook like this? An ex?' She didn't know what made her throw in the last question, but as soon as it came out, she regretted asking it. She realised that she didn't really want to know the answer if his skills had indeed been acquired from one of his ex-girlfriends.

He smiled. 'My mother. She insisted I learn. She said she didn't want me to starve or eat unhealthily when I went away to university.'

'She sounds like a smart lady.'

'She also said that a man who can cook is a chick magnet,' he said teasingly.

Willow burst out laughing.

'Is it working?' he asked.

'*I'm* certainly feeling the attraction.'

Soon enough, they finished dinner and settled on the sofa with drinks. Dominic put on a film called *Tai Chi Master* in the background, which is an old Jet Li movie. Having both seen it numerous times, they spent time making commentary about their favourite parts and comparing the fight styles of the most famous fighters in history.

'Who's the best fighter?' she asked.

'That's easy. Bruce Lee, of course.'

She laughed. 'Well, I guess that's an easy one.' She took a long sip of her wine. 'How about this? Which is the most powerful style in the world?'

'Oh, that's a tricky one,' he said as he contemplated. One of his arms was around her shoulders and she gently stroked the flesh on his arm. 'I'd say Krav Maga.'

'Interesting. Why that one?'

OUTPLAYED

'It's aggressive and you have to target where people are the most vulnerable,' he said. 'Rules are irrelevant and each aggressor doesn't care for the well-being of the opponent.'

'I probably know less about this style than others, but that does sound pretty brutal.'

'I have a question. Which one of them has the best move?'

'Ha!' she exclaimed. 'That one's easy. Capoeira, of course.'

He chuckled. 'And you're not biased at all, I'm sure.' His voice was pure sarcasm.

She sat forward, turned to him and his arm fell off her shoulder. 'Well, *you* said Krav Maga before and you've studied in that one,' she said pointedly. 'And besides, no bias is necessary, sir. It's been proven. Some people at National Geographic were curious about this too and set up a test. They had all the bells and whistles tech. They analysed everything, speed, velocity, force, the whole nine yards. Skilled fighters from Capoeira, Muay Thai, Taekwondo and Karate tested their best kicks. The Taekwondo guy had the most powerful kick, but Capoeira won the contest as it was the one with a kick that used the most effective technique. They said it was something about the highest ratio of force to velocity and highest ratio of mass to acceleration. The technique was the most effective for a single strike.'

She watched as his face creased into an appreciative grin. Her entire body started to tingle.

'Willow, I don't think you'll ever cease to amaze me. How the hell did you find out about that?'

She settled back into his arms as Jet Li kicked butt on-screen with a couple of sticks in a temple. 'Well, you see, I really like a particularly famous capoeirista called Lateef

Crowder. He's frigging amazing! As I follow him, the Nat Geo experiment which he participated in came up in my social media feeds.'

'Ah, I see.'

'He's an actor too. He was in one of the newer *Mortal Kombat* films, kicked a Muay Thai guy's butt in a movie called *The Protector* and he's a body double for the main guy in the new series called *The Mandalorian* from the Star Wars franchise.'

'Are you a secret Trekkie Wookie geek, Willow?'

She could hear the amusement in his voice. 'No secret about it. I'm out and proud. I'm happy to let my freak flag fly.'

'Out and proud, huh? Now that is something I *would* like to see... you *out* and proud.'

Before she realised what he was up to, her wine glass was out of her hand and being placed on the coffee table.

'Dominic, what the... I was enjoying that.'

'I think I know something you may enjoy just a little more.'

'Ah, do tell,' she said, as she felt his hand go to the zipper at the back of her dress.

She arched her spine as her skin was confronted by the cool air in the apartment. Her gaze was pointed at the television, but every fibre of her being was hyper focused on what Dominic might do next behind her. He eased her dress from her shoulders and she heard his intake of breath.

'Bare. You kept those luscious breasts bare for me.'

Her eyes fluttered closed when his large arms came around her and he cupped her breasts. He circled and flicked her nipples until she could be silent no longer. She let out a moan and he squeezed her nipples, which caused her to groan. He lifted her like she weighed nothing and placed her on the sofa in the space between his spread legs.

She tilted her head when she felt his hot breath on the side of her face. She quivered as his tongue came out and licked its way along the curve of her ear. He bit down on her lobe and she yelped with pleasure.

'Lift your sweet arse for me, Will.' He whispered the instruction softly in her ear.

She did as she was told and he hiked up her dress and relieved her of her underwear. She helped him out a bit by shimmying it off her legs. Lifting her once more, he made her sit on his lap, still facing away from him.

'Spread 'em,' he instructed again.

She was putty in his arms as she moved her legs and let them dangle off the side of his thighs. Her core was now fully exposed and she never felt more powerful in her life. She felt one of his hands go back to her breast and the other headed in the other direction. She gasped as his thick fingers touched her most sensitive place.

'*Dominic...*'

'Baby, I love it when you're so wet and ready for me.'

Her head dropped back on his shoulder and she whimpered when she felt him circle her clit. The sensation of his hand on her breast, the other in her wetness and the giant bulge straining against her arse made her feel wild and wanton, and willing to give this man anything he asked of her.

Before she could formulate any more thoughts, he plunged two of his fingers inside of her. The sound that emitted from her throat when he did that wasn't one she recognised as her own. It was deep and guttural, and more primal than she could have ever imagined coming from her throat.

'*That's* right, baby, don't hold anything back from me.'

He kept a steady pace, plunging in and out, and out and in. She groaned and panted and spread her legs even wider for him. He rolled her nipples between his index finger and thumb, and she started to feel the quickening inside. His exploration of her in both her northern and southern regions was more than she could take. She held on as long as she could, but when his two-fingered dives inside her rapidly increased in pace, she lost it. She felt herself clench and then she let out an almighty scream of pleasure and release.

'*Dom...*' she panted.

He carefully lifted her off his lap and laid her out on the sofa, a wicked smirk overtaking his face. There was a predatory look in his eyes as he stood up to his full height and began undressing. Instead of subsiding after such a freaking amazing orgasm, her heart rate began picking up again as inch after inch of his flesh was exposed. He truly had one of the most impressive bodies she'd ever seen. He was cut and ripped in all the right places, no doubt a product of his extensive martial arts training. Halfway through the exodus of his attire, Willow's eyes were drawn to his 'V' lines. She traced their path as they disappeared into the waist of his trouser. Her quick intake of breath revealed how deep her anticipation was for what lay beneath, concealed by only a couple of layers of fabric.

'Dominic, hurry up! This is fucking torture.'

He gave her a sly smile. 'Oh, ye of little patience...'

'Don't you dare spout ancient English at me!'

OUTPLAYED

He chuckled. Then he unbuckled his belt, unfastened his button and slid down his zipper. His jeans fell in a heap on the floor. She took in how his dick strained against the barrier of his white Calvin Klein boxers. Her chest tightened.

'Dominic, you're... *beautiful*...' she gushed.

He raised his eyebrow with an amused look on his face. '"*Beautiful?*" Are you sure that's the best adjective to describe me, Will?'

She sat up and she realised that she was pretty much eye level with the bulge in his underwear. 'But it is. Every inch of your body is beautiful, Dominic. Every toned muscle,' she said, as she traced her hands up from his calf muscles, 'your chiselled thighs, your tight arse, your fucking fantastic cock.' She kissed him through his boxers and he drew in a deep breath.

'Dominic.' She stood in front of him. 'I didn't come into Bar Made that first night looking for... whatever this is.' She watched his brows furrow. 'But I'm glad I did meet you. And I'm glad I came back a week later. This,' she indicated by pointing from him to herself, 'is getting me through a very tough time in my life and I'm grateful for you.'

His brows full-on creased. 'Willow, I don't need your gratitude for fucking you.' His tone was sharp and cutting.

Her clumsy words had made him angry and changed the mood, and that was the last thing she needed or wanted.

'Dominic, I'm sorry. That's not what I meant. It didn't come out right,' she soothed. 'What I mean is, when I'm with you, when you touch me... you make me feel good, *so* damn good! No one has made me feel that good sexually in a really long time.' She smiled. 'It turns out good sex is really good for the soul too. I just feel... better. And that's down to you.'

Slowly, his face softened again and the predatory glint came back in his eyes. 'So, what you're saying is that I'm like your sex therapist?'

She giggled and considered his words. 'Well, not an *ethical* sex therapist, what with the sleeping with your patient, but sure... I guess so. You got right down to the crux of the matter, Doctor, and guided me to enlightenment. You helped me release what was pent up inside me. I'm ready to sing the praises of your brand of therapy to anyone who'll listen. Your groundbreaking methods have really done wonders for me.'

Neither of them could hold it together. They both burst out laughing.

'Well, I've been working on a new type of treatment,' he said. 'It's still very much in its experimental stages, but I think it could get you to the next stage of your recovery. Would you be interested in taking part in my clinical trial, Ms. Blake?'

Excitement bubbled up inside her. 'I trust you completely, Doctor. I know you'd never steer me wrong,' she said with a pout.

With that, Dominic scooped her up and threw her over his shoulder, caveman style, and started walking.

She screamed and laughed. 'Dominic, you ogre, I have legs.'

'Yes, you do, and they're the sexiest legs I've ever had the pleasure of getting my hands on.'

'I mean, I can walk.'

'You agreed to the trial, my sweet Willow. This is part of it. You being vertical is a no-no according to rule number one in the clinical trial. Rule number two is that you should wear zero items of clothing and rule number three is, Doctor knows best.'

OUTPLAYED

He got them to his room and put her on the bed. 'Strip!' he ordered.

She complied without argument, shimmied out of her dress and tossed it across the room.

He followed suit and divested himself of his boxers.

Her eyes widened when he unfurled his ample penis. 'Doctor, what big teeth you have.'

He smirked. 'All the better to impale you with, sweetheart.' Dominic then wiped the amusement off his face as he climbed onto the bed. 'Get on your knees.'

'But—'

He cut her off, 'Rule number three, Willow.'

Once again, she complied, getting on all fours.

'Put your arms on the headboard,' he whispered. 'Hold on tight.'

Willows eyes opened wide and her mouth gaped when she felt Dominic's sudden intrusion in her nether regions. She instinctively dipped her chest towards the bed and pushed her arse up and backwards towards him. She gasped as his wet tongue travelled its way along her folds. She let out a yelp when he began to probe her, hitting just the right spot.

'*Dom... f...uck!* That's... so *fucking* good.' She gasped again and again until she could take it no more. The man was masterful with his tongue, but she longed for even more of him. 'Dominic! I *need* you... Now! *Please*,' she pleaded.

'Rule number three. You should just relax and enjoy the ride,' he said lustfully.

'Relax? You are kidding me. How can I relax when your tongue is—'

Whatever she was going to say was forgotten the moment Dominic replaced his tongue with one, then two, followed by three fingers. The man didn't stop his plunder until another orgasm ripped through Willow, causing her to fear she'd go hoarse with the amount she screamed.

The man barely gave her any time to recover. Just as she started catching her breath and was about to collapse in a heap on the bed, he lifted her arse back up and spanked her. She yelped.

'Oh, no, you don't. Your treatment's not over yet. Put your head and arms on the bed.'

She didn't dare disobey him at this stage. Excitement started building up inside her even more this time. As she lowered herself into position, she felt him briefly leave her and then heard the familiar sound of a foil wrapper.

'*O... ooh... ahh,*' she whimpered, as he eased himself inside her. Somehow, having him enter her from this angle, made it feel even more potent. Dominic was a handsome man. He was chiselled in all the right places, and more importantly to her right now, he was blessed in length and girth and he knew how to use what he'd been gifted.

'*Will...ow...*' he groaned. She was glad that she was not the only one on the brink of losing control. 'Willow, you're so fucking beautiful. I don't think I could ever get enough of this body,' he said huskily.

He eased his way in and then out at a steady pace. Almost of their own volition, her fingers went to her clit and she started circling it. It was too much.

Too damn much.

When he started speeding up, she grasped the bedsheet and started thrusting her arse back to meet him pound for pound. At one point, he nearly pulled out of her completely, but she was not having it. She pushed herself back and re-impaled herself.

'Greedy girl!' he said, amused, and smacked her arse again.

She didn't mind one bit. A few more spanks from him and she found that she was on the brink. 'Dom, I think I'm going to come.'

'That's my girl. I'm right there with you. Come with me,' he said desperately. '*Come...*'

A few more well-placed thrusts and she succumbed. If she thought the other two orgasms he'd given her tonight couldn't be beaten, then she had another thing coming... pun intended... Her body went rigid before the explosion. As promised, he was right there with her. His guttural groan that seemed to go on forever and the tight squeeze he gave her arse cheeks were evidence that he had lost all remnants of control. She felt him jerk repeatedly, which complimented his heavy breathing. Every aspect of what they'd just done together was amazing. That is, until he started to withdraw. If only he could stay there forever, she thought. *If only...*

He left the bed and went to what she could see was the en suite. He then came back and collapsed on the bed next to her, while pulling her back into his chest. 'Willow, you're spectacular!'

'You're not too shabby yourself,' she said with giggle.

'And to think, all I had planned for myself tonight was a bit of Netflix.'

'Well, at least you can say you did the chill part.'

They both laughed until their stomachs hurt. Eventually, all that could be heard from Dominic's room was heavy, followed by softer breathing. Within ten or so minutes of their wild escapade, both Willow and Dominic were fast asleep, content to stay entangled in each other's arms.

CHAPTER 10

- meia lua de compasso -

Willow woke in the middle of the night with a start. At first, she didn't have a clue where she was, but the heavy arm resting on her hip brought it all back. She started having flashbacks of the night before. The memory of every lick and thrust from Dominic had her feeling all tingly inside.

There was a part of her that wanted nothing more than to just lie there and relish in the feeling of comfort this beautiful man was giving her. However, the other part warned of the danger of becoming too attached. For all she knew, this could all come to a screeching halt tomorrow.

He's hot, but he's not yours. And that's all there is to it!

Head screwed back on straight, she tentatively extricated herself from his warmth. It was a painstaking exercise, as the last thing she wanted was to wake him and have him question why she was leaving in the middle of the night... again.

Once she was out of the bed, by the glow of the light that was still on in his living room, she found her dress. When she was at the door, she turned back and looked at him. He'd shifted his position after she moved, but thankfully, he was still asleep. She smiled and pulled the bedroom door gently closed with her on the other side.

She gathered the rest of her belongings and got dressed. Not wanting him to think poorly of her, she rummaged around to find a piece of paper and pen so that she could leave him a note. Items acquired, she sat down on the sofa and got to writing.

> Thank you for an amazing night, Dom. Don't worry, I'm not running away. I just have to be up early in the morning. I'll text you tomorrow. Will.

When she was finished, she opened up the Uber app on her phone. Thankfully, the app said it would only take the Uber a few minutes to get there. With one last woeful look at Dominic's bedroom door, she let herself out of the main door of his apartment. She spent the few minutes she had to wait staring into the now closed Bar Made after she exited the building. The shutters were down, but as she remembered from before, the fish tank was visible in one area of the non-shuttered glass. Seeing the tropical fish illuminated in the glass case took her down a mini tunnel of memories which had her grinning like the cat who got the cream.

'Ah, Dominic... Who knew that stumbling into the right bar on a wrong night could have procured such rewards!' she whispered to herself.

Soon enough, the Uber pulled up and she was homeward bound with a smile still plastered on her face.

⭐

When Dominic woke up, the sunlight was streaming through the windows. This shocked him because it had been a long while since he'd slept straight through the night. He reached over for Willow as his eyes tried to get accustomed to the bright morning light.

Nothing!

He quickly glanced over to where she'd fallen asleep. His eyes widened and his lips tightened in irritation. He shook his head and pulled himself into a seated position. Then, legs planted on the floor on the side of the bed, he stretched out his tight muscles. He was walking around his bed to head for the door to his bathroom, when he spied a folded piece of paper on the floor by the bedroom door. He walked over, flipped it open and read its contents. It was then that he was able to release the tension that had crept into him.

'So, you haven't done another runner after all,' he said with a smile. He placed the message on his bedside table and resumed his journey for the bathroom.

One of these days, I'm going to have to get that woman to spend the entire night with me...

⭐

After Willow got home from Dominic's place so early in the morning, she had a few more hours of sleep. Truth be told, she could easily have stayed over there with him, but fear and weariness had reared their ugly heads and sent her running. She knew she'd call him and see him again, but a big part of her still wanted to keep him at arm's length.

She wasn't totally lying in her note to Dominic, however. Gabriela had said that she'd call her at some point this morning. In the likely event that Gabriela had bad news for her, she preferred to be alone when she heard it. She'd already had breakfast and cleaned the house by the time Gabriela's name flashed up on the screen of her mobile phone.

She took a deep breath as she answered. 'Hi, Gabriela,' she said, trying not to sound too nervous.

'Hey, Willow!' she exclaimed. 'How are you today?'

'Good, thanks.' Willow could hear a lot of commotion in the background. 'Where are you? What's happening there?'

Gabriela laughed. 'Sorry, that's Sean and Carlos playing. When *Papa* is on duty, things get a little wild around here. My husband is like an overgrown child around Carlos. I'm going to go to a quieter room. Hang on.'

Willow listened as Gabriela moved around and eventually settled into a better location.

'Much better. I can actually hear myself think now,' Gabriela said.

Willow chuckled, imagining the 'happy family' scene currently taking place at Gabriela's house. She also felt a pang in her chest. It was a scene that she had long been desperate to have for herself, but she'd realised the futility of such a dream.

Without any more preamble, Gabriela got straight to the point. 'Okay, so I've had a good think and I've decided that I want you to be the new manager of my new baby *La Mesa Duquesa*.'

Willow was stunned into silence. So stunned, in fact, she nearly dropped her phone. She had to scramble to catch it as it slipped from her hand.

'Are you sure, Gabriela? I mean, I don't really have experience in the restaurant industry and just thought... there was no way...' She was rambling and she knew it. She also knew that a thinking Willow would not have said these things to her future employer mere seconds after being offered the job. She had clearly developed a sudden case of 'foot in mouth' disease.

Gabriela burst out laughing. 'You have an interesting way of instilling confidence in a boss.'

'*Shit!* I mean... crap!' Willow covered her forehead with her free hand and closed her eyes for a few seconds. 'I'm so sorry, Gabriela. I guess I was more prepared for you to say "no".'

'Why in the world would I have said "no"? If anything, it was an easy decision. You're vastly overqualified and I'm glad I can snap you up before you get enticed back into the corporate world.'

'There is absolutely no possibility of me finding that life enticing anymore. That world has left a bad taste in my mouth. A fresh start is what I desire most.'

'Well, I'm glad to hear that. You have what I've been looking for, for the last few months. I want someone with drive and business acumen who is a people person. What's equally important to all of that is someone who understands Cuban food and can appreciate what I'm striving for with the *La Duquesa* brand. *La Duquesa* or The Duchess, was my mother. That's what my father called her. He named his club after her and after he handed the reins over to me, I continued to do my best with it in her honour. My mom loved dancing, but she also loved food. She loved to experiment with food from her native Trinidad, but she also learned to make many Cuban dishes so that my dad could also have a taste of home at our table. *La Mesa Duquesa*... or, The Duchess' Table... is for my mom.'

By the time Gabriela finished speaking, tears had started coming to Willow's eyes. 'Thank you for putting your trust in me, Gabriela. I promise I won't let you down.'

'I know,' Gabriela said with a smile in her voice. 'Also, before I forget, in a couple of weeks, it's the Notting Hill Carnival. Every year, at a particular spot near the route, a bunch of capoeiristas from different schools get together and have a huge *roda* and then enjoy the festivities. Are you up for it?'

Willow smiled. This sounded like the icing on top of this call. 'Oh, that sounds amazing. I'd never heard of this before.'

'It is amazing,' Gabriela agreed. 'It's a great opportunity to play Capoeira with people from other schools, and because of the event, we also get a lot of spectators who get interested in Capoeira. It's a blast!'

'Count me in!'

'You could bring Dominic too, if you like. He seemed to enjoy us playing in the park. He'll probably enjoy this too. If not us, then the carnival will keep him plenty entertained.'

Willow grinned. 'You know what, I think that's a great idea.'

'Excellent. How are things going with you two, if you don't mind me asking?'

Willow took a deep breath. 'Okay, I guess. He's a wonderful guy and I like him, but I think I prefer to keep things casual.'

'Ahh... What about him? Is that what he wants? What I mean is, I saw the way he was looking at you. Hell, we all did. Jennifer was already trying to make bets about your future with him.'

'She was doing what?' Willow was stunned.

Gabriela giggled. 'All harmless fun. But Willow, that man looked very invested to me.'

OUTPLAYED

Willow considered what Gabriela had said. 'I don't know about that. Casual is all I think I can handle right now. Plus, with my new job, I'm going to be too busy for anything more.'

'Willow, if you want more from that man, you shouldn't let a damn thing stand in your way. If you want him, you better make time. If he's worth it, you'll know it.'

Willow contemplated in silence. Gabriela made good point, but Willow's recent life experience had made her very gun-shy.

'Sorry, Willow, if I sound a little too ominous. A very good friend of mine, Luna, went through some things and it caused her to shut herself off. She nearly lost someone who turned out to be the love of her life because she was too scared. I saw the way you looked at Dominic too. I can tell you have feelings for him, more than casual ones, even. When you first joined us at *Jogo Arrepiado Capoeira*, you looked haunted. But since Dominic has been around, you've looked lighter. You're more open with us at the school and you smile more. I think he's good for you. But what do I know? Maybe I'm still in semi-newlywed bliss and I'm just being a nosey matchmaker because of it.'

They both laughed.

'Thank you, Gabriela. I think I needed to hear all of that. And I'll ask Dominic if he wants to hang out with us at the Notting Hill Carnival *roda*.'

After they ended the call, still swept up in her new job giddiness, Willow texted Dominic to ask him if he wanted to come to the Capoeira *roda* at the carnival. He agreed enthusiastically after making several highly sexual references which had Willow getting instantly overheated.

SHONEL JACKSON

⭐ *The cake, the icing and now cherry on top... Aren't you a lucky girl today, Willow!*

A couple of weeks later, it was the day of the carnival. Willow had spent more and more of her time and nights with Dominic since she'd invited him to come along. They grew a lot closer and she began to let her guard down. With Gabriela's advice ringing in her ears daily, how could she not?

He'd taken her out on his motorcycle quite a few times, they'd cooked for each other and she reined in her impulse to leave his bed and go home when she woke up in the middle of the night. He'd rewarded her with the best orgasms in the mornings when she stayed. Those orgasms were a great reason to stay. But not just those. Dominic had been attentive and sensitive to her needs. He also kept her in fits of laughter whenever they were together. For the first time in a long time, Willow could honestly say that she was happy.

Willow took a cab to his apartment and they travelled together by public transportation to get over to West London where the carnival would take place. At a certain point along the journey, the trains could take them no further and they had to walk to get to where the Capoeira *roda* would take place.

As they walked through the crowd of carnival goers, they soaked in the atmosphere. People were clad in bright, glittery outfits with the flag of their native Caribbean country draped around their waists or attached to their shoulders, Superman style. The sound of Soca music pumped through speakers, injecting the atmosphere with fire and excitement. People danced in the manner expected at a carnival of Caribbean origin, gyrating, twerking, arms wide open and carefree. Others stuffed their mouths with Rice and Peas, and Jerk

OUTPLAYED

Chicken. Revellers laughed and sang and gave in to the spirit of the festivities.

Willow loved every second of it. At certain points, as the crowd grew denser, she had to cling to Dominic so that they could make their way through and get to their destination. He held on to her tightly and she relished the comfort it gave her to have him there with her. When they got to the clearing in the crowd where Gabriela had told her that the *roda* would be, she spotted many men and women milling about who she was positive were capoeiristas because they wore the brightly coloured, distinctive designs of the *abadas*. A few minutes later, she spotted some of the members of her school, including Gabriela.

'Gabriela!' Willow shouted over the din of the background music. 'Gaby!'

When Gabriela turned and spotted Willow and Dominic, she smiled, waved and ran over to greet them. Her husband Sean trailed behind her.

'Hey! I'm so glad you could make it, and you too Dominic. I like it when Willow brings you around. It seems to always cheer her right up,' Gabriela said conspiratorially.

Willow's eyes widened and then she looked up at Dominic, who had a huge grin on his face.

'Does it now?' he asked with a cocky grin.

'Gabriela! Stop meddling,' chastised Sean good-naturedly. 'Sorry about my wife, Dominic. She came out of the womb nosey. Remind me later to tell you the story of how we first met.' Sean then put his hand out and shook Dominic's. 'Glad to have you. Come, let me get you set up with the *pandeiro*.

That should give these two enough time to gossip before we get started with the *roda*.'

Gabriela slapped him on the arm as he walked off with a grin.

Willow rolled her eyes and reluctantly let go of Dominic's arm as he went off with Sean. She watched as Sean introduced him around the gathered capoeiristas.

'I don't care what you say, there is nothing casual about what is going on between you two. You barely wanted to let him out of your vice grip just then. And the way your gaze follows him... girl, you got it bad!' Gabriela concluded.

'Is it that obvious?' Willow asked with a frown.

'Willow, what's going on between you two is as clear as day.'

Willow wrung her hands. 'It is?'

'Of course, silly. You're in love with him, and by the looks of it, he's not far off either.'

Some women walked past them singing a Soca tune at the top of their lungs and drowned out Willow's reply, so she repeated herself. 'Are you crazy? The ink has barely dried on my divorce papers. *Love* is an inconvenience my life can't handle right now.'

Gabriela looked at her pointedly. 'By what you told me about your ex-husband, it seems that your marriage was over a heck of a long time ago. Take my advice, Willow. I know you've been through a lot but try to leave a little room in your life for magic. I can't think what my life would've been like right now if I hadn't done the same. Sean and our son are the best things that have ever happened to me.'

Willow smiled. 'I'll try, Gabriela, but...'

'No "*buts*", Willow. Just think about it, okay?'

'Okay... I will,' she agreed, but still with some doubt in her tone.

Gabriela grabbed Willow's hand and started dragging her over to the rest of the group.

'By the way,' Willow started, 'what did Sean mean about the way you two met?'

Gabriela giggled. 'Well, you see, what happened was... I was kinda spying...'

'Spying?!' Willow's eyes widened.

Gabriela belly-laughed at the look on Willow's face. 'Come on, I'll tell you later.'

⭐

Dominic said hello to all the people Sean introduced him to and did his best to remember all the names. Sean then showed him the rhythm he wanted him to play on the tambourine. It was simple and Dominic was happy to be given the job. By the time Sean moved away from him to greet different Capoeira practitioners, Dominic had started freestyling with the instrument.

'Hey, you're pretty good on that,' commented Miguel, one of the guys Sean had introduced him to. He was a student from a different school to Sean's. 'You play it like a professional.'

Dominic looked up into the man's eyes and smiled. 'Not at all. I guess I must be a natural.' Dominic was a comfortable six feet tall. There weren't many people whom he literally had to look up to, but this guy was a giant.

'And you don't play Capoeira either?' Miguel asked.

'Nope. I'm just here with my...' Dominic thought for less than a second about how to finish that statement. '...girlfriend.'

What the hell!

He went on. 'Willow's been playing for a long time. She's the professional.'

'Willow?' the man asked curiously.

'Yes,' Dominic confirmed, as he pointed over to Willow, who was still talking with Gabriela. 'Yeah, she's right over there with Sean's wife, Gabriela.'

Miguel looked over to where Dominic pointed. Dominic cast his eyes back over to the other man in time to see the shocked looked on his face.

'You're with *Víbora*? *She's* your girlfriend?' Miguel's shock was very evident.

Dominic frowned. He sensed something else was going on here. 'You know... *Víbora?* I thought you and Sean weren't part of the same school.'

Miguel shook his head. 'Nah, we aren't, but *Víbora* and I go way back.'

Dominic's jaw tightened the moment the words were out of the other man's mouth. '*Do you?*'

Miguel put his hands up in a placating gesture. 'No, *no*, not like that. *Víbora*... Willow is my master's wife. Well... I guess that's ex-wife now.' Miguel's face was full of regret.

Dominic's eyes widened briefly, and then he tried to school his reactions. 'I see.'

'Many people at our school miss her. It's good to know that she's alright. After everything that happened... but I'm sure you know about all of that.'

Keeping a leash on his feelings was hard, but he didn't dare let on that he had no idea what Miguel was talking about. Dominic wanted him to keep talking. So, he grunted noncommittally.

OUTPLAYED

'Anyway,' Miguel went on, 'that's all ancient history now. Treat her right. She deserves better than what *Mestre Lesma* gave her. That was brutal.'

Dominic nodded and tried not to crush the teeth in his mouth as he ground them.

They both turned when someone started playing the *berimbau*. Dominic remembered that Willow had told him about this bow-like instrument. She'd said that it was the most important of all the instruments in Capoeira, and that by the tone that guy was playing it in now, it meant that it was time to start the Capoeira game in the circle, or as Willow had schooled him, in the *roda*.

'Come on Dominic,' Miguel said, taking his own tambourine from the backpack he had on his back. 'You're over here with us.'

Putting the nuggets Miguel had inadvertently spilt out of his mind the best he could, Dominic followed him and joined the other three musicians who were already in their places in one area around the circle.

CHAPTER 11

- aú pesado -

Zum zum zum
Capoeira mata um
Zum zum zum
Capoeira mata um
Onde tem marimbondo?
zum zum zum
Onde tem marimbondo?
zum zum zum

The colourful Capoeira trousers blended in perfectly at the carnival. Tantalising reds, vibrant blues, lush greens and mesmerising yellows sliced through the air as the capoeiristas showed off the best of their craft. In any other context, this could be called a performance. Some might say it was the theatre of the fighting arts. However, this theatre was not for the faint of heart. There were no beginners present in this *roda*. Today, right in the middle of the biggest street party that celebrated Caribbean culture in the U.K., there were two dozen or so highly trained martial art experts executing moves with such precision that spectators gasped often, likely thinking that someone could get hurt. If they did think that, they wouldn't be wrong. Playing in a Capoeira *roda* carried with it its own unique thrill. It was a feeling that could never quite be explained. However, the energy created inside it was like a living, breathing entity, that stayed with the capoeirista long after the *roda* ended.

Willow took in the sights, sounds and energy of the *roda*. A huge crowd of carnival goers had gathered around and were enjoying the spectacle. Some of them had slotted themselves in the gaps of the circle. The children were wide eyed as they grinned. This wasn't the first time Willow had seen this kind of reaction to a *roda* that took place in public, it had just never happened for her in the middle of a carnival. Somehow, however, it worked. It made sense to have their *roda* take place in the midst of this giant, energy ball of revelry.

What she hadn't expected was to see *Palmeira*, or Palm Tree. She hadn't seen him since she left her old Capoeira school. But there he was, right next to Dominic, towering over him, playing the *pandeiro*. Seeing her present and her past like this had jolted her a little after she and Gabriela finally stopped gossiping. He was a good guy and had been a good friend to her when the proverbial shit hit the fan in her former relationship. But when she'd finally walked away from both her marriage and her old Capoeira school, she'd felt like everyone was against her. So many of their friends from the school had taken Ricardo's side in the debacle. It had caused Willow's guard to go all the way up. She'd built the wall high and airtight. Now, seeing Miguel again out of the blue and with a little more hindsight, she realised that she'd left some casualties in the wake of her great escape from Ricardo and most of the things that reminded her of him. She'd left a good friend who hadn't deserved the way she'd ghosted him when he'd frequently tried to call and check in on her.

Willow made eye contact with Dominic as she walked around the *roda* to enter the circle from next to the musicians. She smiled at him and he smiled back, but there was something else in his eyes which she could not place. For a second, her stomach twisted, but the energy of the *roda* quickly brought her back to the present.

She entered the *roda* with an *aú*. She played against a man who, by the skills he displayed, was one of the higher-ups in his own school. Willow didn't know him, but she enjoyed their game together. After a few minutes of energetic play, the man gave her a hug and started to depart the circle. Someone then tapped her on her shoulder from behind to signal that they wanted to play a game with her. She was standing on the edge of the circle at the time. She was happy to play another game, so she stepped forward to allow them room to enter. Then she turned around. The person who entered the *roda* took her breath away, but not in a good way. Her chest and jaw tightened and she wasn't sure she could keep the look of distaste from her face. Involuntarily, she cast her eyes over to Dominic and she swallowed. There was a look of concern on his face as he continued to bang away on the *pandeiro* in perfect rhythm with the other four musicians.

Willow watched as he glanced over at the new man that had entered the *roda*. She knew Dominic didn't know this man, but then an expression crossed his face that she'd never seen before. In an instant, she was positive that Dominic had guessed who the other man was. There must have been something on her face that'd given it away. Maybe it was her disdain, her distaste, her fury... Who knows, but she felt it in the tightness in her chest and in the way she clenched her hand. All around her, two dozen capoeiristas sang, clapped and gave their energy to the *roda*. Meanwhile, she felt frozen to the spot.

'Willy!' the man who wanted to play her shouted.

She remembered a time when she'd actually been fond of that nickname. She'd thought it was endearing. Now, it made her want to spit. Willow knew that it must have been only seconds since the man touched her on her shoulder, effectively tagging himself into the game. However, in her mind, it was like those seconds had dragged on for hours, by the number of things that passed between her and the man.

The Capoeira master on the lead *berimbau* abruptly changed the rhythm and song that he played, snapping her out of it. He selected one that had a much slower tempo. Whether she liked it or not, she was about switch from playing the more up-tempo and energetic Capoeira Regional, to the much slower and more intimate Capoeira Angola with her lying, adulterous ex-husband, Ricardo *'Mestre Lesma'* Santos.

Capoeira de Angola
Capoeira de Angola, ai meu Deus
eu falo de coração
eu jogo a Capoeira
pois é minha obrigação
o mestre que dá lição
na roda de Capoeira
dou um aperto de mão
Camaradinha
viva meu Deus
le viva meu Deus, câmara
viva meu mestre
le viva meu mestre, camara

SHONEL JACKSON

The song that the master chose to sing was particularly poignant though. It was about a person who plays Capoeira because they have no other choice, as it was in their heart. It also says that in the *roda*, that person, the master, will give you a handshake. It then goes on to say, 'Long live my master who taught me', as the chorus of voices of the other capoeiristas echo back the sentiment.

Mestre Lesma had indeed taught her and he'd been a good master of Capoeira for her, but in his base persona, as Ricardo, he had hurt her deeply. When he offered his hand for her to shake, she saw blue murder. This was the battle that raged on inside her as she shook his hand anyway, and put on her game face to start doing the *ginga*.

Ginga is Capoeira's most fundamental movement. Other martial arts had a base stance, but hers had a base movement. The player would repeatedly step on invisible triangular points as they swung their arms back and forth as if they were continuously protecting their face from potential attacks. *Ginga* is a grounding movement and that's what it did for her in that moment. It grounded her and calmed her fury. It was never a great idea to bring uncontrolled emotions into the Capoeira *roda*. It could get someone badly hurt.

The music washed over Willow as she moved and weaved her way in and around *Lesma*. The style her past and present schools practiced was Capoeira Regional. The movements for that tended to be faster, with powerful kicks and sensational acrobatics. Most Regional schools would also dabble a bit in Capoeira Angola, which was the older and more traditional style. These movements were slower and bodies came into much closer contact at a slower pace. Legs swept along arched torsos, arms could brush chests and players practically breathed each other's air due to their proximity. To the casual onlooker, this closeness could appear to be quite sensual or even sexual to a perverted few. Willow prayed that Dominic didn't think so. She shoved that thought away the moment it made an appearance. Her mind needed to be clear to play well.

Lesma swept his right leg along the left side of her body, and she responded by letting her body swing down in the direction his kick was going, ending in a squat. She then countered by slowly swinging her own right leg up and along his body.

The twisting, turning, weaving, and gliding of body parts continued to the end of the song. Just before a new song started, *Lesma* struck. When she was in a vulnerable position with one leg outstretched, he got under her and swept her supporting leg out from under her. Simultaneously, he grabbed her arm to ease her inevitable fall. She ended up on her back, but it was with careful placement from *Lesma*. She was annoyed with herself that she didn't see his move coming, but that's the way it went in the *roda*. And, if you were playing against a master, they would almost always take advantage of your vulnerabilities, if only to make sure you learned something.

Lesma then offered her his hand. She took it and then he pulled her back up to standing. She met his eyes, this time with resolve instead of fury, nodded and then walked out of the *roda*. She went over to Miguel, who was still playing the *pandeiro* next to Dominic. She offered to take over playing the instrument and he handed it to her. Miguel smiled and had a look of understanding in his eyes.

Before Miguel joined the rest of the circle, the giant bent down and said into her ear. 'Dominic seems nice. You deserve a good guy.' With a wink and a gentle squeeze to her arm, he entered the *roda*.

On the parade route, there were large trucks decorated with banners and followed closely by members of their band. These people were scantily clad to differing degrees in different flamboyant costumes. They danced and revelled to their heart's content to the Soca music blasting through giant speakers. There was one band that was covered in what looked to be chocolate. It was slathered all over their faces, bodies and clothes. This seemed kind of crazy to Dominic, but what he couldn't fault was the absolute sense of abandon which emanated from each and every one of them. He hadn't been to the Notting Hill Carnival for years, but he did remember always having a good time whenever he came.

This time was no different. Everything about it was great, the atmosphere, the music and the beautiful woman that was currently gyrating her arse on his crotch. He was nowhere near her level of dance skills, but he could more than hold his own. He held on to her hips and grinded into her. The next thing he knew, Willow was back up to standing and facing him. She threw her arms around his neck and wined her waist, once again against his now bulging cock. This was like sweet torture.

He smiled darkly at her audacity to do this to him when they were out in public and he could do little to placate his throbbing hard-on. He rocked along with her as he held her eyes. He had no doubt in his mind that they were both thinking the same thing.

OUTPLAYED

It had been over two hours since they'd left the Capoeira group hand in hand. As they walked away from the *roda*, he'd had a strong urge to ask her about everything Miguel mentioned, but he knew that it was neither the time nor the place for such a conversation. A final glance around the Capoeira players had proven fruitful. Ricardo, Willow's ex-husband, had daggers for them. The other man was tall and well built, but Dominic knew he had a few inches on him. Watching Willow play against this man in the Capoeira *roda* and to see her body in such close proximity to him had driven Dominic crazy. He knew this method of doing the martial art was not unusual. He'd seen videos of this style and there was also a bit of this when he'd gone to see Willow in the park. Seeing this human scum, as Dominic surmised, near his woman, and she was *his*, knowing what Willow had said he'd done to her, had him struggling to keep the rhythm on the tambourine.

He'd seen Willow stiffen and the furious and slightly frantic look in her eyes when she turned and saw the man, and he'd just known without a shadow of a doubt that that was the ex. He was the S.O.B. who'd driven her into a bar, all alone to drink away her troubles. For a split second, Dominic had thought that maybe he should have a smidgeon of gratitude for him, because if it weren't for Ricardo's idiocy of fucking things up so royally with this amazing woman, Dominic would never have met her. The smidgeon was gone the same instant that it came when he saw the way Ricardo leered at them from a few metres away. Even though he had another woman's hands wrapped around his arms, trying to get his attention, his gaze was still planted on his ex-wife and the hand she had clasped in Dominic's. Thankfully, Willow didn't seem to notice the standoff as she'd been engrossed in conversation with her friend Miguel.

When Willow finally let him come up for air, Dominic glanced to his right. Sean and Gabriela had decided to come and revel with them. He couldn't say for sure, as Willow had had his full attention for the last few minutes, but he would bet good money that Sean and his wife had been similarly engaged as he and Willow had just been. Sean's face was as flushed as Dominic was sure his own was, and Gabriela's back was pressed up to his front, with her head resting comfortably on his shoulder. He didn't know the couple well enough yet, but he had a gut feeling that they were good people and he was glad that Willow had them in her life.

'Hey, Willow,' Gabriela shouted over. 'Should we keep following along the route or do you want to go get some food?'

'Food please,' Willow yelled back. 'I'm starving!'

Both of the women burst out laughing and Dominic watched as a knowing smile crossed Sean's face.

'Me too! I can't believe I've lasted this long. Come, there's a Jerk Chicken stall over there,' Gabriela said, pointing in the direction of the food. 'And it's not too busy at the moment.'

'You boys hungry?' Willow asked.

Dominic met Sean's eye and they both nodded in agreement.

'Get me whatever looks good, babe,' Sean said to his wife.

'The same,' replied Dominic.

'Alright, stay here. We'll be back,' shouted Gabriela as they ran off.

OUTPLAYED

When the women left, Dominic and Sean did that thing that men do when they're at a party and suddenly find themselves without their dancing partners. They nodded along with the music and made idle chit-chat.

'Thanks for coming and giving your energy to the game, Dominic. It was appreciated,' Sean said, over the loud music.

'I hope I didn't mess up the rhythm too bad. I tried to keep up with the professionals.'

'Nah, you were great.'

Both Dominic and Sean looked over to where the women were ordering the food. Unbeknownst to them, they both carried similar expressions on their faces. They were 'silly happy' ones.

'Hey, Sean, you mind if I ask you a question?' Dominic asked.

'Sure, go ahead.'

'That guy, the one that Willow was playing Capoeira with, tall, well-built... is he some kind of a master or something?'

Sean thought for a second. '*Lesma*? Yeah, he's a master. I met him a few times when we visited other schools for events.'

'Is his real name Ricardo?'

'Ah, I think so. To be honest, I use the Capoeira nicknames for most of the players I meet outside of our school. It's how we mostly introduce ourselves. Why do you ask?'

'I'm almost positive that that guy is Willow's ex-husband. I just wanted to confirm it before I talk to her about it. I don't want to risk bringing up some of her demons if it's not him.'

'Ah, I see,' Sean nodded.

SHONEL JACKSON

Dominic watched as realisation entered Sean's eyes. Willow had clearly shared some things will Gabriela, who had then filled her husband in too.

'Okay, let's see.' Sean appeared to search his memory. 'Now that I think about it, Willow transferred over to us from the school *Lesma* is the master of, so...'

'And Willow told me that her ex-husband is her former Capoeira master.' Dominic's jaw tightened once more as he remembered the way Ricardo took her legs out from under her and then pulled her up when she was on the ground in the Capoeira *roda*.

'*Shit*, sorry, mate. Did Willow know he was going to be there today?' Sean asked remorsefully.

'No.' That much was clear by the look of shock on her face earlier.

'Is she alright?'

'Not sure. I'll talk to her about it later. I didn't want to ruin her good time by asking,' Dominic replied.

'Good idea.'

Before either of them could say anything else, the ladies sauntered back over, bearing treats.

'Look what we have,' Gabriela announced.

Dominic took in the ecstatic look on Willow's face and he was glad he hadn't brought up the subject of her ex-husband with her earlier. The man had ruined enough of her days.

★

By the time they made it back to Willow's house, it was nearly four in the morning. Dominic and Willow had partied with Sean and Gabriela until well after the carnival ended and they ended up at an after-party. He didn't remember the last time he'd had that much fun. Getting to spend time with the other couple was definitely a highlight. Sean had spent much of their time together taking playful jibes at his wife, who had held her own and happily reciprocated.

'Damn, I'm exhausted. I haven't partied that much in ages. I'm not sure I'll be able to function tomorrow,' Willow said as she giggled and tried to get her key into her front door. 'Thank God I'm still kinda unemployed and have nowhere to be in the next twenty-four hours.'

'Speak for yourself pretty lady,' he said as he followed her in and closed the door. 'I have an order of stock coming in for the bar around lunchtime, so, hangover or not, I've got to be there.'

She giggled even more as if she found his predicament enormously amusing.

'You think that's funny, do you?' he asked slyly.

She turned to him as she was about to make her way up the stairs. 'You know what, I kinda do.' Then she playfully stuck her tongue out at him, turned and ran up the stairs.

Dominic's eyes widened, then he smiled and shook his head.

Where has this woman been all my life?

From the very first night he'd met her, she kept him on his toes. Everything she'd done had surprised him. And just when he thought he'd never ever see her again, there she was, shocking him. He had a flashback of the first night she'd let him kiss her... touch her... He remembered the look in her eyes as she lay on the table in his bar while he drove into her. He realised in that moment that that was where he always wanted her. Not necessarily splayed out in his bar, but he wanted her to always look up at him like that as he claimed her for himself, and himself alone.

Dominic wasn't ready to fully delve into why he suddenly felt like that. That was soul-searching that was better left for an entirely different day. Tonight was for taking Willow again just to see that look in her eyes once more.

He slowly shrugged out of his jacket and made his way to the kitchen to get himself a glass of water. He was parched, so he drank two. Then, he went back to the stairs and took them one at a time. He made his way along the corridor to her bedroom door. It was slightly ajar. He pushed it open and the sight that awaited him put a smile on his face and caused the beating thing in his chest to flutter. Laying tucked under the sheets was Willow, face scrubbed clean of makeup. She was breathing deeply and evenly, making adorable little snoring sounds.

You have got to be kidding me!

As much as he wanted to sink into her, seeing her like this also made him happy. He'd seen far too many looks of anguish on her face since he'd met her for him to begrudge her this moment of pure peace.

He went into her en suite and got undressed, folding his clothes and leaving them neatly on the corner of her wide countertop. He stopped when he caught sight of himself in the mirror. What he saw was a man with a goofy, happy look on his face. He couldn't remember the last time he looked or felt like this. He would have to be an idiot not to know the source of this newfound goofiness.

On impulse, he decided to jump into the shower. It was a long, cool one and it was just what he needed. He got out and dried himself off with a towel from Willow's supply in her bathroom cupboard. That shower helped to clear away some of the cobwebs he hadn't even realised he'd been carrying around with him. Then, back in the bedroom again, wearing only his birthday suit, he slid into the bed next to Willow. He pulled her back into his chest. She fit perfectly. She made a little cooing noise and then settled. Before he drifted off into sleep, Dominic realised that he was exactly where he always wanted to be.

CHAPTER 12

- macaco -

The next morning, Willow wasn't sure, but she could have sworn the reason she woke up when she did was because of whatever that was poking her in her back. As she came around and became aware of her very familiar surroundings, she stretched out some of her achy muscles. When she realised what was poking her, she smiled and slowly turned around, being careful not to wake Dominic. Lifting the sheet, her supposition was confirmed as she cast her eyes at the shaft which was standing at attention. She chuckled, which caused Dominic to stir. She froze and peeked up at him. He didn't wake but turned over onto his back and settled again. When she finally dropped the sheet, she nearly cracked up. Dominic's number one lieutenant had left a giant tent in her sheet.

Never one to look a gift horse in the mouth, Willow made a decision then and there. It wasn't like she had much of a choice in the matter. As soon as she felt the familiar pressure on her back and saw the evidence of it under her sheet, she could feel herself getting wet. Reaching into her bedside table, she pulled out a foil wrapper and took out the condom inside. She bit her lip as she contemplated how she could possibly do this without waking him until she was ready.

⭐ With the utmost precision and care, she took hold of him and ever so slowly, rolled the condom down to cover every glorious inch of him. At that point, she was throbbing and salivating about what she was about to do. She eased out of her underwear and bra, which she'd fallen asleep in, and thanked her lucky stars that Dominic was a deep sleeper.

Dominic was having the best dream ever. The comfortable haze encircling him made him sure it was a dream. The star of it was none other than Miss Willow Blake herself, the sexy-as-hell, kick-arse vixen. She was beautiful and had him burning up with need. He could not get enough of her and he was sure he never would. He knew he was dreaming and the absolute last thing he wanted was to wake up. After all, he was so damn close to coming.

However, something caused him to snap his eyes open. At first, he was confused, but when his mind started to clear, he realised that what he'd been experiencing over the last few minutes was no dream. Willow was bobbing up and down on top of him and it caused her perfect, pert orbs to bounce mesmerizingly in front of his eyes. Her arms were flung behind her head, which was thrown back too, and her mouth was agape as she moaned unabashedly.

'Willow, what the...' He couldn't get anything else out as he succumbed to the sensations rippling through his body. Now that his dream haze was clear, he was being engulfed by an equally pleasing haze which had him wanting more. He'd experienced a lot in his life, but never anything like this.

SHONEL JACKSON

Waking up to find himself being ridden by the most beautiful woman he'd ever met was new and very much welcomed.

She was close. He could see it in the tight, short pants that were being sucked from her. He was there with her. Even though he'd been partly unconscious when this all started, clearly his dick didn't have such qualms. He was rock hard and almost ready to explode. He raised his hips, held on to hers and met her pound for pound. His release was epic and hearing her bellow his name as she found her own climax had him digging even deeper to try to eke out every drop from her.

Eventually, Willow collapsed on top of him, her heart pounding against his. 'Good morning, handsome. I hope you liked your wake-up call.'

He couldn't help it as a laugh ripped through him. Encircling her in his arms, he kissed her on her forehead. 'Good morning, my sexy Willow.'

Their laughter had an entirely less-welcomed consequence, however. As he was pushed out of her, he rolled over, taking her with him. When she was flat on her back, he propped himself up on one elbow. 'Well, that was an interesting way to wake up,' he said with a chuckle. 'Not that I'm complaining, but I feel like I missed the start of the party and arrived just in time for the last dance.'

She smirked. 'One might argue that that is the best part.'

He considered what she said. 'You know what Willow, *one* might be right. And what a final song it was.' He lowered his head to hers and took her lips in a sensual, all-encompassing kiss which left him breathless and turned him on all over again.

OUTPLAYED

Dominic's taxi pulled up outside his bar about ten minutes before the delivery van got there. He knew that he'd been cutting it far too close, but it was almost impossible for him to drag his arse out of Willow's bed. Never mind a viper, the woman was a vixen and had somehow managed to enchant him with her beauty, wit, intelligence and sweet pussy... not necessarily in that order. Her early-morning surprise had led to him taking her two more times before professional preservation finally kicked in and he managed to tear himself away from her.

So, as he received his order of multiple kegs of lager and bitter and checked off the order he'd placed with what had arrived, the only face that kept running through his mind was that of a feisty beauty called Willow. Even when the burly delivery men who usually delivered to Bar Made looked at him in a weird way and asked if he was feeling okay, as he'd apparently had a goofy smile on his face the entire time, he'd simply smiled even more and carried on ticking off items on the clipboard in his hands.

He was feeling happy and he knew it. He wasn't used feeling like this and he wasn't quite sure what to do with himself. The last meaningful relationship he'd had with a woman felt like it was a millennium ago. His last long-term girlfriend had been like a wrecking ball in his life and had left a very bad taste in his mouth. While he was a man who believed staunchly in monogamy, every other woman in his life after the wrecking ball had received his monogamous attention for no more than a handful of dates. He'd stayed faithful, but quickly moved on. He'd had no desire for anything more serious than that.

SHONEL JACKSON

Now, here was Willow with her badarse Capoeira sexiness making him hard the moment he first laid eyes on her. Seeing her kick that drunk's arse that first night had him feeling like she was some kind of kindred spirit. Not because she'd beat someone up, but because she knew *how* to and only used her skills when she'd had no other choice. In essence, she was perfect! He, on the other hand, had been stupid. He'd let her walk out of the bar that first night as he'd proverbially been left with his tongue hanging out. When she shocked him by coming back, he was determined to let 'stupid' rue the day it reared its ugly head. She'd let him get her a drink and let him take her out for dinner. When she let him touch her, he'd thought that he was the luckiest man in the world. Being inside Willow Blake was a spiritual experience, one that he was keen to have continue.

When his stock was fully stored, he headed up to his apartment with the intention of getting in a few hours in his gym. Just as he grabbed a bottle of water to take with him, his mobile phone started ringing from inside his jumper pocket. He was fully aware that he still had a stupid grin on his face and that it had grown even wider as he pushed his hand in his pocket hoping that it would be Willow calling him. It wasn't, but his smile remained, nevertheless. It was his older sister Joy requesting a video call.

'Hey, baby bro!' Joy exclaimed when they connected.

'Hey, J!'

Dominic had a good relationship with his sister. More so than just siblings, they were good friends. He was also close with her seven-year-old daughter Ruby. In fact, Ruby had called him her favourite uncle more than once. It was irrelevant to him that he was in fact her only uncle, as Joy's husband Thomas only had sisters. It was the sentiment that counted.

Joy eyed him suspiciously. 'What's going on with you?'

Dominic frowned. 'What do you mean?'

'Your skin is flushed and your eyes are smiling.'

One of his eyebrows raised. 'And you don't like it when my eyes are smiling?'

'Don't be a smart arse, Dom. For months, you've been broody as hell, a real grouch. Now you answer the phone looking like you're happy to see me.'

He laughed. 'Sis, I'm *always* happy to see you.'

'Don't be silly. I know you're always happy to see me. However, that fact hasn't been obvious on your damn face for ages. I know something's up and you might as well tell me now, because you know I'm going to find out anyway.'

Dominic shook his head with a grin.

'You win the lottery or something, bro?'

He thought for a second. '*You could say that,*' he said slowly.

Joy chuckled and seemingly decided to play along. 'How much did you win?'

'The jackpot,' Dominic replied cryptically.

'You're freaking me out, bro. What the hell is going on with you?'

Dominic propped himself against his kitchen island and mulled over his sister's question. On one hand, he wasn't sure he was ready to share Willow with any member of his family just in case he jinxed it. He wasn't a superstitious man, but he didn't want to do anything to push his luck. On the other hand, Joy was relentless. The woman was known to bring grown men to their knees without even breaking a sweat. He realised that telling her now, at least the CliffsNotes version, might be the lesser of two evils.

'Well,' he started, 'I met someone.' He then braced himself for the onslaught.

Joy's eyes widened and her mouth gaped. '*What?*' When the surprise wore off, a wide grin took up residence on her face. '*Really?* Who's the lucky lady that has my broody brother looking like a giddy schoolboy?'

'Her name is Willow.' He didn't dare share her surname. Both Joy and her husband had friends in high places. He didn't doubt for a second that she would go snooping if she could. 'I met her when she came into the bar one night.'

Well, that part was true.

'Are you serious, Dominic? Since when do you start chatting up customers? I thought doing that was a hard and fast "no" for you.'

'It is.'

'Then what happened? She must be something real special for you to charm your customer away from her friends when she's on a night out.'

Dominic shook his head while simultaneously passing his fingers through his hair. 'She came in alone.'

Once again, Joy's mouth gaped open. 'You chatted up a woman who came in to drink alone? Do I detect a little desperation, little bro?'

Dominic rolled his eyes. 'She's nice, J. She's funny and exciting and the night she came in, she was having a bad day which got worse when some drunk idiot started harassing her. She put him in his place, then left. I barely got her name before she was gone. I didn't think I'd ever see her again. Then, a week later, she came back, and we struck up a conversation.'

'Ah, so you'd left an impression on her even though she was there and gone in a flash. There's the Dominic that I know and love,' she said teasingly, 'always charming the you-know-what off the ladies!'

He grinned. 'Not quite.' At this point, he didn't care how much she teased him.

'I'm happy for you, Dom.'

Suddenly, Joy's eyes opened wide again. 'I know! Bring her over this weekend. Any woman who can bring that goofy look to my brother's face deserves an invitation.'

'I don't think that's a good idea, J. This is new and I don't want to overwhelm her.'

'Don't be silly, Dom. Is she skittish or something?'

'No. Not at all.'

'Then what's the problem?' she asked with a raised eyebrow.

Dominic had seen that look a thousand times.

'Tell you what... how about we leave it up to her? Tell her your favourite, beloved sister Joy is extending an invitation to you both and that I'd be honoured if she considered coming. We'll go with whatever she decides.'

'You really do know how to lay it on thick, J.' As he said this, he remembered that his sister's cunning knew no bounds. He knew that she knew he would feel obligated to ask Willow. He knew his sister well enough to know that she hoped Willow would also feel obligated to come.

'Joy?' He smiled, feeling resigned to his fate. 'I know that, as you work for that super hush-hush government agency, you can't really tell us about the specifics of your job, but I swear, you deserve a promotion. Well played, J. Well played!'

'I'm sure I have no idea what you're talking about, dear little bro.'

'*Sure*. Anyway, I've got to get my workout in before you con me out of my bank details or something.'

She laughed. 'Don't be silly, Dom. I have no reason now to try to con that out of you.'

'Thank you.'

'I've had it since the day you opened your account at sixteen.'

Eyes wide with shock, Dominic opted not to get sucked into Joy's web any further. He was only half sure she was joking.

'Goodbye, Joy. Stay out of trouble.'

'Don't I always?'

'No.'

'See you two on Saturday.' She grinned devilishly.

He knew the futility of challenging her on this point, so he let it slide and instead ended the call with a shake of his head while making the sign of the cross.

As he settled into his workout, Dominic wondered what Willow would say to Joy's invitation. 'Well, there's only one way to find out,' he muttered to himself as he tapped on the incline setting on his treadmill and started making his way up Mount Everest.

★

After Dominic left that morning, Willow had busied herself by tiding up her place and then going out shopping. She'd gone through some boxes in her attic that she used to store her corporate gear. She'd surmised quickly that almost all of it was unsuitable for her new position at *La Mesa Duquesa*. Those clothes were far too formal and they reminded her of a time in her life that she'd rather forget. Her shopping trip had proven fruitful and she'd come back home with bags full of slacks, casual blouses, pleated shirts and accessories.

As she waltzed around her room with some of her new things, she heard the notification tone for an incoming text message chime on her phone. Upon inspection, she saw that it was her friend and new boss.

> Gabriela: Are you as hung over as I am? I haven't drunk that much since before Carlos was born, and breast feeding made drinking a no-no. My head feels like I took one of the steel pan players from the carnival home with me, shrunk him and implanted him and his pans inside my brain!

Willow cracked up when she read Gabriela's stream of consciousness.

> Willow: I think I'm in a lot better shape than you. No steel pan players over here.
>
> Gabriela: If I didn't like you so much, I'd hate you!
>
> Willow: Lol
>
> Gabriela: Anyway, I wanted to check if you had some free time this week? I want to give you a tour of the restaurant and get the contract signed. I'll send you a digital copy first, of course.
>
> Willow: Yep, I can meet you pretty much anytime. Jobless, remember. Or at least I was! Lol.

Gabriela: Haha! How about tomorrow? After lunch? I have to be at the club in the morning, then I need to meet the interior designer at the restaurant as well.

Willow: That's fine by me!

Gabriela: Perfect! See you then!

Willow: See you!

⭐ Willow put the phone down and headed across the room to her closet. She'd barely finished putting a new top on a hanger when her phone started ringing. Wanting to continue putting away her new things, and figuring Gabriela wanted to have a more detailed chat, Willow slipped her Bluetooth earphones out of her pocket and put them into her ears. She did this without going over and looking at the phone screen. She tapped on one of the devices in her ears to connect the call.

'You forget something, babe?' Willow answered.

Dominic had his mouth open, ready to greet her, but was made mute by the endearment. Then, the small smile on his face vanished with Willow's subsequent comments.

'Hello? Are you there, hun? Did you forget to say something in your texts just now? Shit! Are these things even working? Crap! I just put my Bluetooth in and...' Willow rambled on, but Dominic still hadn't said anything.

Babe... hun... texts just now...

He felt a flash of hurt and anger as he realised the endearments weren't meant for him, as he knew he was not the one who'd been texting her *'just now'*.

He finally decided to speak. Even though Willow could have just been texting sweet nothings with another man, he realised that there was nothing he could do about it. Neither of them had really put a label on what was going on between them. Then he remembered that he had called Willow his girlfriend when he met her former Capoeira classmate Miguel at the Notting Hill Carnival *roda*. It hit him that it was only he who'd said it, not her.

'...can't hear me... I'll go grab my mobile and switch the Bluetooth off.' Her voice was a little breathless.

'I hear you, Willow,' he finally said before she could disconnect her device. He could hear the dryness in his tone.

'Dom! It's you! I thought my wireless was malfunctioning. I couldn't hear you before.'

'It was probably just a bad connection at first. I hear you fine now. What are you up to?'

'I went new-job shopping. I'm just putting everything away.'

'*Oh...?*' It was all he could manage. It was pathetic and he knew it. It took everything in him not to ask her who '*babe*' and '*hun*' were. Sudden insecurity had him questioning if he had the right to.

'Dom, is everything alright? You sound strange.'

'Yes... yes, everything's fine. Ah...' He decided to go for broke. 'Who were you texting with?' He did his best to make his question sound casual.

'Huh?'

'You said you were texting someone *just now*.' He couldn't help but put a strained emphasis on his final words.

'Oh, you *could* hear me.' She laughed. 'Thank God! These earphones were bloody expensive and I only bought them recently.'

'Er... well?' He really needed her to get to the point. He didn't know where the sudden jealousy came from, but he needed an answer A.S.A.P. If she was seeing someone else, he'd rather find out now, before he got even more sucked under her beautiful spell. 'Who?' Another attempt to sound casual.

'Oh, yeah. That was just Gabriela. She wants me to go see the restaurant. You know what, I think she may still be drunk from last night!'

Willow's laughter floated through the line to him and for the first time since their call connected, he fully let go of the breath he had a stranglehold on.

'You know what, Dominic? I can't wait to start this new job. My life has been a nightmare for so long, this job could mean a new start for me!'

Dominic hadn't been to church in nearly two decades. That scripture life had never really been for him. However, right then and there, an apt Bible quote came to him... *'The Lord giveth, and the Lord taketh away'*. His relief at hearing that she wasn't referring to another man as 'babe' was quashed the moment he heard her describe her new job as the thing that heralded in the start to her new life. He suddenly felt deflated.

'I'm happy for you, Willow. No one deserves this more than you.' He may have started feeling a little shitty, but he meant every word of that. He wanted the best for her.

Then, another thought occurred to him. It crossed his mind that he was just overreacting. They were new. They didn't need labels yet. There was something good between them and he should just take things one day at a time.

This new thought taking root, he perked up a bit. 'When are you going to the restaurant?'

'Tomorrow afternoon.'

'How about I come pick you up afterwards and take you for an early dinner? There's something I want to ask you.'

'Oh... I'm intrigued! What is it?'

He smiled. 'Nope. Not saying. I can only ask you in person.'

'Has anyone ever told you that you were a tease, Mr. Made?'

'Once or twice.' He grinned. Her easy laughter was enough to pull him completely out of the funk which had descended on him. 'Okay, I have to get downstairs and open the bar. I'll see you tomorrow.'

'See you tomorrow.' The softness in her tone warmed him. 'And Dominic?'

'Yes?'

'Thank you.'

'For what?'

'For being the other thing in my life that's kept me sane and smiling recently. It means a lot to me.'

He felt his chest tighten as he forced himself to keep his tone even. 'I'm glad I could help. Gotta go. Bye, Will.'

'Bye, hun.'

By her sudden, sharp intake of breath, Dominic could tell that she hadn't meant to use the endearment. It would be an understatement to say that Dominic went through the rest of his night walking around on cloud nine.

✯

It was a slip. She hadn't meant to call Dominic 'hun'. But when she got comfortable around people, she often used the friendlier language. She liked him. She knew that he knew that. She wasn't lying when she'd told him that he'd kept her sane.

The last thing she thought would happen when she walked into the bar that first night was that she'd meet someone. The man had come out of nowhere and crash-landed into her life. Plus, the sex... It was like he was in her head. He knew what she wanted without her having to say anything. Saying he was the best she'd ever had was an understatement.

However, this scared the shit out of her. They hadn't discussed labels for whatever it was between them. A small part of her was still gun-shy. She'd been badly burned and had little enthusiasm for more than just sex with anyone. But when she was with Dominic... that hot burning flame inside of her dared to hope. After Ricardo, she knew hope was a dangerous thing to have, but her emotions were being very uncooperative at the moment. She liked him... a lot. She wanted him... a heck of a lot! He seemed to want her too. But she'd been wrong before.

As much as a part of her wanted to keep him, another, equally potent part of her wanted to run. It was an instinct she fought daily. She didn't want to play games with him, so she'd forced herself to try to take things one day at a time. Even just now, using the endearment at the end of the call sent a streak of fear through her, plunging her into a state of 'what ifs'.

Shaking her head and taking a deep, cleansing breath, she carried on putting away her new things, recognising that the tiny ember of hope inside her had grown significantly since she'd first met Dominic Made.

CHAPTER 13

- meia lua de fente - esquiva -

A surge of excitement ran through Willow as Gabriela showed her around *La Mesa Duquesa*. The restaurant was stunning. It was smoky-grey and accented with gold highlights. Modern sconces were strategically placed in key locations along the walls and on pillars to give the perfect amount of mood lighting. It added an ambiance that could not be beaten, in Willow's opinion. The thing that was yet incomplete was the flooring. As a result, there were workmen still busy making measurements and laying the rich mahogany floorboards. Willow knew the finished product would be jaw-dropping. Of this, she had no doubt.

The kitchen, however, was complete, which is where Gabriela was leading her now. 'Gabriela, this place is amazing! You've done such a good job.'

'Thanks, girl. This place is my fourth baby and I really want to get it right.'

'Fourth?'

Gabriela laughed as she pushed the kitchen door open. 'My precious baby is of course Carlos. My sexy baby is the best man I've ever met. My club, *La Duquesa*, is my father's baby which he dedicated to my mom but handed over to me. And this,' she said looking around the stunning kitchen, 'is the professional baby of my dreams. I've created everything here from the ground up and worked my arse off to get it here. It's my time away from Sean and Carlos, which I wouldn't have done if it weren't so important to me.'

'I'm happy for you, Gaby.' Willow smiled at the woman who had quickly become a very good friend to her. She remembered the times when Gabriela would ask her to hang out after Capoeira lessons and she'd refuse. Willow had been suspicious of everyone's motives back then. In fact, if she was honest, a part of her still was at times. Getting burned by her ex as well as a woman whom she'd considered a friend had devasted her and sent her down a truly dark path of self-loathing and distrust. When she'd walked into that lawyer's office after psyching herself up to sign the divorce papers and get on with her life, and then seen her former friend Priscilla sitting there with that smug smile on her face... Well, Willow had nearly lost it again and let rage take hold of her. The last time she'd let that happen, neither she nor Priscilla had come away unscathed. Though, Willow's wounds were more emotional, as opposed to Priscilla's physical ones.

It took Gabriela bringing a tall, burly, middle-aged man wearing a chef's jacket over to her to snap her out of her reverie and back to the present.

'This is Cedro. He's the best Cuban chef in all of London. I stole him away from his last gig and I'm never letting him go. I'll chain him to the walk-in freezer if I have to.'

OUTPLAYED

They all burst out laughing at this and Willow wasn't entirely certain she was joking. Gabriela was very determined when she wanted something.

'Cedro, this is Willow Blake, *La Mesa Duquesa's* new manager.'

Cedro approached Willow and planted a kiss on both of her cheeks. '*Encantado*,' he said in a lightly accented voice.

'Pleased to meet you too. It smells great in here. What are you making?' Willow looked around the large, professional, chrome kitchen to see that there was all manner of ingredients on the counter and multiple pots and pans going.

Cedro glanced behind him. 'Testing out a few things for the menu. Seeing what works. Refining some classics too. There's some *ropa vieja*, *vaca frita* and *arroz con pollo*. Tamara, the pastry chef will be back in a minute. She's working on some treats too.' Cedro then left them and headed back over to his duties.

'Gabriela, I'm salivating,' Willow said.

Gabriela grinned. Nobody is better than Cedro. We can try out some of this when he's done.'

'I can't wait!'

'Alright, let's leave him to work his magic and we'll come back in a bit to reap the rewards.'

With one last deep inhale, Willow followed Gabriela out of the magical kitchen. They walked all around the restaurant and Gabriela pointed out many notable features about the place as they went. They also went to into the basement which was partially converted into as large storage area and a wine cellar. There was a shipment of wine that had just come in that morning and Gabriela beamed as she pointed it out to Willow.

'I'm so happy that I'm going to have these on the menu. They are from *La Bodega Martínez*. Remember I told you about my bestie Luna who was also a student at *Jogo Arrepiado Capoeira*?'

Willow nodded. 'Yeah.'

'Well, her husband and his family have produced phenomenal wines in Spain for generations. When I tried some of it a while back, I knew I had to have it on the menu if I was ever able to open the restaurant of my dreams. They are also going to come to London for the grand opening. I can't wait to see them. Plus, Carlos can't wait to see their daughter Lexi. Before they moved to Spain, the kids were inseparable.'

'Oh, excellent! I look forward to meeting them. Jennifer has mentioned Luna so often that I feel like I already know her. It'll be nice to finally put a face to the name.'

The next stop was the office, which was on the upper floor, to sign the contract. Work was still going on up there, so they had to navigate around decorators. As Willow had already read the contract, all that was needed was for both of them to affix their signatures. After going over a few more housekeeping things, they were happy to head back downstairs to the magical kitchen.

⭐

With her new contract in her handbag and a smile on her face, Willow exited *La Mesa Duquesa*. She couldn't help but feel a sense of euphoria. Even though she hadn't been hard up for a job thanks to careful saving over the years, now that she was officially gainfully employed, she couldn't help but feel like the jagged edges of her life were smoothing out a bit.

OUTPLAYED

She loved everything about the restaurant. The *pièce de résistance* was of course the food. Chef Cedro's food was mouth-watering. As for Chef Tamara's take on some very popular desserts in Cuba, *arroz con leche* and *buñuelos*... needless to say, Willow felt gastronomically spoiled.

In a matter of weeks, the place would be open. Gabriela had briefed her on how she'd like to see things run and the marketing campaign that had been well underway for months. There would be joint promotions with the club on occasion, but other than that, the restaurant would be Willow's territory. In the days to come, Willow would have to train newly hired staff and give her input on all matters that would crop up. Willow couldn't wait to get stuck in.

Willow jumped into a black cab not far from the restaurant and decided to call Dominic. An idea had just occurred her and she wanted to see if he would go for it. However, after ringing several times, his phone went to voicemail, so she decided to leave a message instead.

'Hey, Dom! I'm on my way home now from the restaurant and the chefs have overloaded me with a ton of leftovers, including dessert. I know you wanted to go out, but I was wondering if you wouldn't mind coming over to my house instead. I've also got a couple bottles of amazing wine from the restaurant I can treat you with. How does that sound? Let me know.'

With a smile to herself, she finished recording her message and ended the call.

★

Any time he spent with Willow, Dominic had come to believe was time well spent. Upon hearing her voicemail, he was more than happy to go along with her suggestion. After ignoring multiple calls from his father, he'd decided to put the phone's ringer on silent so that he could focus on work. He had a hell of a lot of paperwork to get through in his office and the man's constant attempts to contact him today were unwanted at best.

When he turned onto Willow's driveway, he heard loud music blaring. The lights were on in her living room and he could see straight through her net curtains. He then saw something that almost stopped his heart. The music that she was playing was the cheesiest of cheesy pop. He recognised the song, but he knew he wouldn't be caught dead singing it. Willow, it seemed, did not have such qualms. Through her window, he could see her tearing up the floor and singing into an object he was positive wasn't an actual microphone.

He smiled as he took off his lid and ran his fingers through his hair. Helmet in hand and not making an attempt to hold back his chuckle, he knocked on the front door of her red brick, Victorian home.

To his joy, her singing didn't abate when she opened the door. He couldn't lie, she had a great voice, and right at that moment, he was sure her neighbours could hear her too. The woman was singing that damn pop song, by that artist dating that American football player, and she looked as beautiful as ever as she did it.

Just then, his chest tightened as he slowly exhaled his held breath.

Fuck!

As she grabbed his hand and yanked him inside, he felt his heart pick up speed.

Holy fuck!

OUTPLAYED

This thought started to play on repeat in his head as Willow shut her front door and shoved him up against the back of it. Without a word, the woman pulled his head down and pushed her tongue down his throat. He, of course, was a willing recipient. It hadn't been that long since he'd last kissed her, but any amount of time was too damn long in his book. He pulled her closer with his free hand and felt her melt into him. This was quite possibly the best kiss he'd ever had in his life. Never before had a woman made him feel weak in the knees.

He spun them around and only broke away long enough to put his helmet on the hallway table. With fire in his blood, he came back to her, put his hands through her hair and put his tongue back where it belonged. He didn't know how long they went at it, but when he finally came up for air, his body tingled and he felt a little light-headed.

Fuck!

There that thought was again.

This fucking woman!

'Willow,' he rasped. 'I hope you know I *fucking* missed you!'

Her jaw dropped and she blinked uncontrollably. He could tell that she was holding her breath.

'You... missed me...?'

The uncertainty that crossed her face nearly broke him.

She has no idea, does she?

'But—but we saw each other yesterday?' She stumbled over her words.

His lips quirked. 'And?'

When he felt her gently push against him, he let her off the hook and allowed her to step out of his embrace.

'And... I don't understand why you would miss me.' She threw this over her shoulder as she started in the direction of her kitchen. 'You must be starving. Come on, let's eat.'

Oh no, you don't. You're not going to get away that easily!

He followed her into the kitchen and didn't once take his eyes off her as she fussed around dishing up food and pouring them wine.

'Don't do that, Willow.'

'Don't do what?' She barely glanced up from her task.

'Don't play with me, woman.'

'I'm not,' she said as she poured carefully.

He came closer and sat himself down on the other side of the kitchen island.

'Willow, can't you see I'm trying to tell you something?'

She picked up his plate and put it in the microwave.

'Willow,' he called gently.

She turned back and looked at him. He didn't like the fear he saw in her eyes.

'Tell me you know I'm crazy about you.' He spoke in earnest.

Genuine shock crossed her eyes. 'Ah...'

'I don't expect you to say anything. I just wanted to put it out there. You're one of a kind and I'm glad I was so pissed off with my father that the best thing for me was to sit in my bar one night and consume copious amounts of alcohol. If I hadn't made that poorly thought-out decision, I might not have had the opportunity to meet the most beautiful, feisty woman I've ever met. And yes, I've missed you, a day or no. What, haven't you missed me?' He smirked.

OUTPLAYED

She opened her mouth to speak, but she was saved by the bell as the microwave bell went off.

'Don't you dare!' His voice was gruff. 'Did you miss me too?' His eyes pinned her to the spot.

She nodded slowly and whispered, 'Yes.'

'Was that so hard to say?' he asked, a cheeky smile appearing on his face.

'Kinda...' she said softly as she put his steaming plate down in front of him.

He chuckled. 'I'm not surprised.'

She took out some food for herself and put it in the microwave. As the appliance hummed, she gave him his glass of wine.

'Dig in before it gets cold.'

He nodded and started eating. She followed suit and sat down on the stool next to him after she retrieved her plate.

'I know that that was hard for you to say, Willow. But I need you to trust me. I'm not him. I'm not going to hurt you.'

Then, she did something he hadn't expected. She picked up her glass and practically downed her wine before leaning over to kiss him on the cheek. Then she went back to eating her food. Dominic realised that he was wrong in his assessment earlier. That last one there, *that* was the best kiss he'd ever had in his life.

★

The next morning, Willow woke up with a smile on her face and the remnants in her mind of the sweet dream she'd had. With her eyes still closed, she recalled that in her dream, Dominic had made slow, dirty love to her and had driven her to the point where she forgot her own name. When her mind cleared, she realised that it was definitely a case of a dream imitating life. What the man lying next to her right now had done to her body and mind all night, perhaps deserved a chapter in the *Kama Sutra*.

'Beautiful!' Dominic said huskily.

Her eyes flew open to see that Dominic was propped up on his elbow staring intently at her. She felt her face heat. 'Morning...'

'Morning, Beautiful.'

'How long have you been staring at me, you weirdo?' she mock chastised.

'You think I'm weird because I can't take my eyes off you?'

'Well, no... but I must look awful – hair a mess, morning breath...'

'I couldn't give a damn about any of that. To me, you are perfect!'

Willow felt her entire body start to heat under his gaze and what seemed like adoration.

'Willow, I need to tell you something,' he said tentatively.

He sounded serious and her body tensed. He must have noticed it because he put his arms out and drew her towards him. He left just enough space between them for her to be able to look into his eyes.

'Don't look so worried. What I have to tell you is nothing bad. I'm just worried about how you're going to take it.'

She frowned. 'How *I'm* going to take it?'

'Yes.' He smiled. 'I'm not sure you're ready to hear this. You're a little prickly sometimes, don't you know.'

She giggled. 'Well, you're going to have to tell me now, and whatever it is, I'll try not to freak out.'

OUTPLAYED

With his fingers stroking her naked hip, he spoke. 'Willow, I realised something last night when I pulled up on my bike and saw you through the curtains bustin' a move to Taylor Swift.'

She smiled and asked him hopefully, 'You're a Swiftie too?'

'Oh, God, no!' he exclaimed with disgust. 'My niece is. She enjoys torturing me by using her cuteness to make me watch clips of something she calls *Eras*.' He shrugged and shook his head.

She cracked up. 'You mean the *Eras* Tour? I wish I could have gone to see—'

'Willow... I love you.' His voice was serious. 'Despite the fact that you have terrible taste in music, *I love you.*'

She blinked rapidly, trying to make sense of what he'd said. 'You... *what?*'

He smiled, showing off his perfect, white teeth. 'Willow Abigail Blake, *I... love... you...*' He pulled her in and gave her a kiss on her parted lips.

'But...' She was having trouble collecting her thoughts. Both joy and fear gripped her heart in that moment. 'You *love*... but...'

'Willow, *please*, I don't want you to say anything now. You've been through a lot over the last year and you've not too long ago finalised your divorce. I know you're not ready to say something like that to me. That's not why I said it. I told you because *I* was ready to say it. I haven't felt this kind of connection with anyone for a really long time. You make me happy. I also love that you're a smart arse.' He touched her cheek. 'Baby, you're the only woman I want. You're the only woman I'm ever going to want. You've ruined me for anyone else.' He chuckled. 'You're stuck with me.'

'Dominic, I...' She was very hesitant.

'I mean it, Willow. You're not ready say it back. I know you're not. I promise you, there's no pressure. I already know in my heart how you feel about me, and that's enough for me right now, I promise. I just needed you to know. If you're ever ready to say something like that back, then I'm all ears. If not, then I'm still not going anywhere. I'm here because I love you and want to be with you. Only you. Do you hear me?'

Willow looked at him in wonder. Who was this man that had stumbled into her life, this man who treated her like a queen, a man who she sensed would do anything for her? Even with all of that, she was scared. She was scared to surrender her heart again, but hearing him say that he loved her, made her feel happier than she'd been in a very long time.

'You're right.' She smiled and she could feel that her eyes were watering. 'I'm not ready.' She kissed his soft lips and then pulled back. 'But I'm happy you told me. It... makes me feel... good. I'm scared... I... Thank you for loving me. God, that sounds so stupid,' she admonished herself. 'An amazing man tells me that he loves me and the best I can say is "*thank you*".'

He chuckled. 'Are you kidding? I love your answer. You also said that I was amazing. What more could a guy ask for?' He kissed her again and then rolled off of the bed, giving her a wonderful view of his toned arse. 'Come on. Let me make you breakfast. I have an invitation to tell you about and I need you to be well-fed before I tell you about it.'

'An invitation?' she repeated, pulling the sheet around her as she got off the bed. 'From whom?'

OUTPLAYED

He turned around and paused before retrieving his underwear. The man's glorious penis was beginning to salute her.

'Hey, I'm up here,' he said, signalling for her to raise her eyeline.

Shaking her head, she met his eyes with a wicked smile. 'It's not my fault you're so distracting.'

With a smirk, he finally put on his boxers and walked out of the bedroom.

CHAPTER 14

- chapa - rasteira -

Willow gently tightened her grip around Dominic's waist as they sped through and out of London. They were heading to Kent, a county to the south-east of London, known as The Garden of England. They were very much on the tail-end of summer, but the landscape looked stunning just the same. The verdant hills were breathtaking and it sent a thrill through Willow. On the long expanses of land, she could see horses, sheep and goats. It was a very calming sight and that was doing her a lot of good. She was excited to be spending the weekend with Dominic's sister Joy and her family, but a part of her was nervous about it too. She hoped Joy liked her because she loved being a part of Dominic's life.

She could still hardly believe that he'd told her that he loved her. At this point, she didn't know what she would do without him, but she still couldn't bring herself to say those three little words which, despite what he said, she knew he wanted her to say back to him. No matter what, he supported her. He made her laugh and made sweet love to her in a way she'd never imagined possible. Quite simply, Dominic Made was the perfect man for her. Yet... she couldn't tell him what she knew he more than deserved to hear. She was a hot mess emotionally and she knew it. Her arsehole of an ex had really done a number on her.

After about an hour and a half on the motorway, they exited and headed into a more residential area. He'd told her that they were heading to Royal Tunbridge Wells. From what she could see so far, it was beautiful. She smiled under her helmet and gave Dominic one final squeeze as she settled in for the last part of their journey.

⭐

'Uncle Dummy!' squealed the very high-pitched voice of Dominic's seven-year-old niece, Ruby, as she came running out the front door of Joy's lush home. He'd just helped Willow off the bike and was about to put the bike on its stand when he heard Ruby's voice. He'd barely crouched down to her level before the little girl threw herself at him.

'Hey, baby girl!' he said as he gave her a bear hug.

'You're late. You were supposed to be here twenty minutes ago.'

Dominic eased back and looked at the indignant face of his niece, whom he loved so much. 'I'm sorry, Rubes. We got stuck in a little traffic.'

He watched her little face frown before she turned it upside down to look at Willow.

'You're Uncle Dummy's girlfriend, Willow. I like your name. I'm Ruby.'

Willow crouched down. 'I like your name too. It's beautiful.'

Suddenly, Ruby threw her arms around Willow's neck, which made her become off balance and they both ended up sprawled on the driveway in fits of giggles.

'Ruby! What are you doing to Willow?' came Joy's stern, melodic voice from the front door.

With a laugh, he lifted Ruby off of Willow and placed her back on her feet. He then held his hand out to Willow to pull her up. When she was up again, he pulled her into him and gave her a not so short kiss.

'Ooooh,' swooned Ruby.

'So, this is the woman who's got my brother so lovesick,' said Joy as she approached, echoing her daughter's swooning.

Dominic rolled his eyes and then gave his sister a hug. He watched the light in his sister's eyes as she looked Willow over.

'You're right brother, she's beautiful!'

Willow blushed and then smiled. 'Pleased to meet you,' she said, stretching out her hand to shake Joy's. Joy, of course, ignored this and gave Willow a tight hug. Dominic saw the tension ebb out of Willow's body as she gave into his sister's embrace. His chest tightened with emotion as he bent down and took out their things from the saddlebags of his Harley. They were only going to be here for one night, so there was no need for more. He knew his sister would supply anything else they needed. He could already tell that Willow and his sister were going to get along just fine.

'So, who's hungry?' Joy asked.

'Meeeee,' shrieked Ruby, as she bolted back through the front door.

'Give me strength with that niece of yours!' Joy said with exasperation. 'Alright, come on. Thomas has the grill going in the back. We've got the outdoor heating going if you get cold, Willow.'

For the next two hours, they all ate, drank, joked and at one point, Joy even brought out the family photo album. She took delight in showing a picture of Dominic at about five years old, running butt-naked through the family garden as he tried to escape their mother.

Joy laughed wholeheartedly. 'The boy *hated* the water. Whenever our mother tried to give him a shower, it would prompt a war in the house. One of us always had to go chasing after the little terror.'

Dominic shook his head. 'One thing you'll come to know about my sister is that she grossly exaggerates. That probably happened only about a handful of times – tops!'

'Me? Exaggerate? *Never!*' said Joy with a face full of mischief. She laughed, took a sip of her wine and then focused her attention on Willow. 'So, Willow, I've just realised that I haven't yet asked for your version of how you two met. Dominic was frustratingly vague.'

Willow and Dominic looked at each other and then burst out laughing.

'Ooh, I sense there's definitely a story here. Come on, let's hear it,' she encouraged.

'Well, it's pretty boring actually,' Willow offered.

'Now, who's exaggerating?' Dominic challenged.

Willow stared him down with mock irritation. 'It is,' she emphasised.

Joy's eyes moved between them, tennis match style, as they bickered.

'Joy,' Dominic said, looking at his sister pointedly. 'Willow assaulted a guy!'

Joy's mouth gaped open in shock. 'She... *what?*'

'What's as...sot...ted?' Ruby asked, as only a seven-year-old could.

'Nothing honey,' said Joy quickly, attempting to distract the curious child. 'It... ah... means to help someone.'

With Ruby's nod, all the adults at the table hoped that that would be enough for the child's burning ears.

Willow leaned over to where Dominic was sitting at the circular garden table and swatted him on his leg. '*Dominic!*'

He laughed. 'If you don't agree with my abridged account, then you tell it.'

Willow took in a deep breath and recounted the event to Joy and her husband, taking care with her choice of words in the presence of the child. When she finished, Joy and Thomas looked disbelievingly at each other. Joy spoke first. 'Bad arse! Leave it to you, little brother, to find a lady who can kick butt just as much as you can.' Joy then looked at her husband, mischief in her eyes. 'Babe, who do you think would win in an arse-kicking contest, Willow or Dominic?'

Thomas, with a twinkle in his own eyes, said, 'Well, let me see here. Having seen Dominic take down men almost twice his size and remembering how he pretty much threatened me not to break his sister's heart when we first started dating... I would have to say – Willow. I'm sure she could kick his arse without even breaking a sweat!'

The entire group, including Ruby, burst out laughing. Dominic gave Thomas a pointed look. 'You know what, Tom, I have to agree with you there.' His eyes met Willow's and they sobered. 'Willow has skills that are unmatched by any other and I'm pretty sure she could knock me over with a feather if she so chose.'

Something passed between them then. It was electric. It sizzled. Dominic was positive he was not the only one that felt it. He looked deeply into her eyes and mouthed the words, *I love you*. He turned back to his sister as he took a sip of his beer. Willow reached over and put her small hand on his thigh. He felt her gentle squeeze and then her warm palm as she left it there. It wasn't an 'I love you' back, but right then and there, it was better. Whether she realised it or not, she was seeking him out. Seeking to make and keep a connection with him. He knew without a shadow of a doubt, it wouldn't be long before she felt compelled to tell him exactly what she felt for him. Of this, he was certain.

⭐

The next morning, Willow awoke to the sound of chirping birds and a slice of light coming through the curtains at the window. She was also aware of the feeling of peace that had engulfed her. The physical embodiment of that peace was the finely honed muscular man that had curved around her naked back with his hand placed possessively on her thigh. She could feel his gentle breath as it caressed the back of her neck. She could tell that he was still asleep. He deserved it. He'd taken out all the stops last night. He'd made love to her all through the long night. As they were not in either of their houses, she had endeavoured to keep the noise down. It'd been difficult, but it added another inexplicable nuance to their lovemaking. He had stroked, caressed and suckled on her until she thought that she would spontaneously combust from the pleasure. Hands down, Dominic Made was the best lover she'd ever had. It wasn't even close. It seemed like he knew her better than anyone else had. He knew her without even trying. She was scared of how much she needed him.

With a deep breath in and out, she gently extricated herself from him and sat up on the side of the bed. She looked down at him and smiled. He looked like he didn't have a care in the world. His breathing was even. He was at perfect peace.

As she watched him, she started to feel something akin to anxiety bubble up in her stomach. She knew she couldn't stay in the room any longer, lest her restlessness wake him up. She grabbed some clothes from their overnight bag and went into the adjoining bathroom. After taking care of her morning ablutions, she got dressed in a white t-shirt and multi-coloured *abadas*.

When she re-entered the bedroom, Dominic was still fast sleep, but this time, he had turned and was facing away from her. The sheet covering him had slid down and left his luscious arse on display just for her. It took everything in her not to strip and wish him a 'good morning' the way he deserved. Alas, she grabbed her phone and let herself out of the room, walked through the still-quiet house and headed to the kitchen. A glance at her watch told her that it was just after seven. She grabbed a bottle of water from the fridge and let herself into the garden. It was quite large and long, so she headed down to the bottom, as she did not want to disturb any of the sleepers. She put her water down in a corner next to a bush and started scrolling for a playlist on her phone. When she found what she was looking for, she pressed 'play', turned up the volume and placed the phone down on a large decorative stone.

OUTPLAYED

The device injected the gentle, metallic clanging of the *berimbau* into the tranquil morning. The musician played beautifully and with reverence as he bent the *berimbau* to his will. As he strummed, she gently stretched. She worked through the muscles from her neck to her toes as the sound of the *berimbau* baptised the morning air.

As the instrumental ended, so did her warmup. Then, the track changed. This time, the *berimbau* signalled a new rhythm called the *Benguela*, which held sway over Willow's heart. The capoeirista's melodic voice took hold of Willow and she let it.

A Benguela chamou pra jogar
A Benguela chamou pra jogar, capoeira
Em cinco de fevereiro
Do ano de setenta e quarto
Esta tristeza aconteceu
Na cidade de Goiania
Mestre Bimba faleceu
A Benguela chamou pra jogar
A Benguela chamou pra jogar, capoeira

The *Benguela* is a slow, ballad-like rhythm created by the father of the type of Capoeira that Willow practiced, *Mestre Bimba*. This rhythm is unlike the faster-paced ones *Bimba* created. When capoeiristas play to the *Benguela*, both players' goal is to play beautifully, or *jogo bonito*, as Capoeira players liked to say. Capoeiristas brought their beauty A-game to the *Benguela* and played in a way that demonstrated fluidity and the extent of their skills.

Willow played what could be called 'shadow Capoeira', not unlike what would be called 'shadow boxing'. She moved through kicks, takedowns and dance-like movements, playing off of her invisible opponent. She let each of her sweeps honour

Mestre Bimba. The song recounted the sadness of the community after *Bimba* died at the age of seventy-four and the *Benguela* rhythm of the song commemorated both his birth and death.

Willow was so absorbed in the flow of her movements for the thirty or so minutes that she'd been going for, that she didn't notice the two sets of eyes that were observing her from the garden patio. One was the proud set of the man who loved her and the other was the fascinated one of the adorable seven-year-old by his side.

Ten minutes later, Willow stopped to take a water break and wiped the sweat from her forehead. As she did, the beautiful flora at the back of the garden caught Willow's eyes. Even in the tail-end of summer, Joy's garden was still going strong. She couldn't help it, so she reached out her hand and gently touched the bright-yellow petals of a flower she knew she would not be able to name. She smiled and took another long sip.

'Almost as beautiful as you,' came a voice Willow knew she would always be able to point out in any crowd. She turned and let her smiling eyes meet Dominic's.

'You flatter me,' she said as she grinned.

'Just being honest.'

It was then that Willow took in Ruby, who was clinging to her uncle's side.

'That was so cool! Can you teach me?' Ruby pleaded.

Willow's mouth dropped open and her eyes flicked over to Dominic. 'Ah, well... I don't know. I think maybe you should ask your parents or your uncle first.'

OUTPLAYED

Dominic laughed. 'You have my permission. I'm positive her parents won't mind. They've had her doing Karate since she was four.'

'*Oh! Wow!* You've got a little fighter on your hands,' Willow said. She was genuinely pleased to hear this about Ruby.

'How come you're using music. Karate doesn't have music. I wanna use music in Karate too. Do you think my *sensei* will let us use music in his Karate class, Uncle Dom?'

'I don't think so, Rubes,' he said. 'I think Capoeira is the only martial art that uses music.'

Ruby screwed up her face. 'Capa— what...?'

Dominic chuckled and then enunciated. '*Ca-po-ei-ra*... Capoeira.'

'Capoeira,' repeated Ruby, a lot more careful and correct this time. 'Please, Auntie Willow, can you teach me some Capoeira.' Ruby looked at Willow earnestly.

However, Willow could only manage a dumbfounded look back. 'Ruby, I'm not your aunt, so you don't have to call me that.'

'Yeah, but, one day when you and Uncle Dom get married, you will be my auntie then, so I'm just starting earlier.'

The very exacting logic of what the little girl said couldn't be argued with as Ruby seemed so certain. The last thing Willow wanted was to crush her, but she didn't want Dominic to get the wrong idea. She glanced at Dominic and instead of seeing a reflection of the look of fear she was sure she had plastered all over her face, his showed nothing but amusement.

'Your uncle and I aren't getting married, Ruby,' Willow said, as she tried to clear her throat.

SHONEL JACKSON

'Well, maybe not now, but definitely one day.' The strength in the little girl's declaration belied no uncertainty.

'What makes you so sure?' Willow was genuinely curious.

'Are you kidding? That's exactly how my parents look at each other. Uncle Dom can't stop looking at you! Every second, there he is!'

At this, both Willow and Dominic burst out laughing.

'What can I say, Rubes? She's gorgeous!' Dominic said.

'And then there's all the *kissy*, *kissy*, *kissy!*' She shook her head and then began demonstrating some of her own Karate moves. 'Check this out.' Then Ruby expertly executed a high kick.

'Wow! That was great, Ruby,' Willow said.

Then, after a few more kicks, Ruby stopped and looked thoughtful. 'And another thing. When you two have a kid, can it be a girl? Boys are smelly.'

Both Willow and Dominic's eyes met. Neither of them could formulate words at that moment. Meanwhile, Ruby continued happily showing off her Karate kicks. With butterflies in her stomach, Willow changed the subject and successfully distracted Ruby from this train of thought. The three of them spent the next little while demonstrating their martial arts prowess. Willow taught Ruby some Capoeira moves and the child lapped it up. She caught on quickly and kept insisting that Willow teach her more and more. Even Dominic requested to be taught a few Capoeira moves. Willow definitely relished bossing him around and took delight in adjusting his stance. Soon enough, Joy called them in to have breakfast. When they went in, she'd laid out eggs, bacon,

OUTPLAYED

sausages, toast and steaming cups of tea, coffee and warm milk for Ruby.

⭐ As she stuffed her mouth with the delicious food, Willow took in the scene before her. They all joked and interacted with ease. They were definitely a close-knit family. This was something that she sorely missed in her life. Her heart ached for it and she was almost too scared to hope that some of those things that had come flying out of Ruby's mouth so easily earlier, would come true.

It was late evening when they got back on the road again. Dominic had called Jamal, who was the de facto manager at Bar Made, to let him know when he'd get back in town. While he didn't have to work tonight, he was going to be closing up the place.

As his Harley tore up the road, and Willow's arms tightened around him, Dominic smiled inside his helmet. It had been a great weekend. Seeing Willow interact with such ease with his family solidified in Dominic even more so than before what she meant to him. His family already loved her and he knew that there was no way he was ever going to let her go. In the grand scheme of things, he knew they hadn't known each other long, but he knew he'd do anything for her. He just had to get her to realise that it was okay to let go and let herself feel everything he could see so clearly in her eyes. He knew that she wasn't playing games with him. Her scars just went deep. Patience was the name of the proverbial game here.

⭐

As soon as they walked into the very busy bar, Dominic saw him. In fact, as he held the door open for Willow and let her precede him in, the back of his father's greying head stood out like a Jack-in-the-box. After having a phenomenal weekend with his family and his lady, the absolute last thing he wanted was a confrontation with his sperm donor. Because that's all the man had ever really contributed to his life. After gifting Dominic 50 percent of his DNA, Malcolm Made had physically and emotionally checked out of parenthood.

Stopping Willow before she could go too far into the bar, he said, 'Will, my father's here.' He indicated the grey mane of the man in the dark-brown leather jacket.

She turned to him with a smile in her eyes. 'Really? I'd love to meet him. I mean, if that's alright... if you want me to. If he's anything like Joy and Ruby, I'm sure I'll love him too.'

Dominic's jaw tightened. He hated to burst her bubble, but after carefully avoiding giving too many details about the man whenever Willow asked about his parents, Dominic realised that this time, he had no other choice but to get into it.

'I promise you, you won't. We're not close and for very good reasons. I'm just going to have to apologise to you now.'

Willow's face fell and her brow knitted in concern. 'Apologise for what?'

Dominic shrugged. 'He tends to bring out the worst in me.'

With one hand occupied with their overnight bag and his helmet, Dominic used his free hand to pull her into him. He gave her a long, almost desperate kiss. Keeping their eye contact, he stroked his finger gently along her cheek. He smiled and took in a deep breath. 'Come on. Come meet the man who spawned me.'

She frowned, but she let him lead her over to his father, who was sitting at the bar sipping on what was more than likely

OUTPLAYED

Dominic's not-so-secret stash. The man had no boundaries. While Jamal would never serve anyone else from Dominic's top shelf bourbon, he always gave in whenever the old man showed his face around here.

'Dad, what are you doing here?' Dominic said when they were standing right behind Malcolm. His tone was stern and full of judgement. He knew that his tone had shocked Willow. He could feel her hand tighten in his as he held on to hers. He didn't want to risk scaring her away, but he also wanted her to know all of him, the good, the bad and the daddy issues.

Malcolm slowly swivelled in his chair and plastered a charming smile on his face to greet his son. However, the ship had long sailed on the times when Dominic fell for that smile hook, line and sinker.

Glancing down at Dominic's hand holding Willow's, he said, 'Dom, is that any way to speak to your father? Especially in front of this beautiful lady.'

Mentally, Dominic rolled his eyes. He didn't give an inch. 'What are you doing here, Dad?' Dominic repeated.

'I came in looking for you and Jamal said you'd be back soon, so I waited.'

'That doesn't answer my question,' Dominic said tersely.

Ignoring his son, Malcolm, turned his attention to Willow. 'Since my son has clearly forgot his manners, I'll introduce myself.' Grasping Willow's hand out of Dominic's, he said, 'I'm Malcolm Made, Dominic's father and the man he named his bar after.'

Dominic couldn't help the venom in his voice as he ground out every word, 'I did not and would never name my bar after *you*. I just used my surname.'

'Well, you got that from me, didn't you?'

Dominic had never felt this close to violence in his life, but right now... well, only his father could bring him this low.

Ignoring his son again, Malcolm refocused on Willow. He still had her hand in his. 'And you are?'

Willow glanced at Dominic before she answered his father's question. 'I'm Willow, Willow Blake.'

Malcolm kissed her fingers. '*Enchanté.*'

'Nice to me you too, Mr. Made,' Willow said, politely.

'Call me Malcolm,' he said, with all the charm of a second-hand car salesman. 'Dominic, why didn't you tell me you're seeing such a beautiful lady?'

'And why would I have done that, Dad? You're not her type.'

'Dominic!' Willow was aghast.

'Mind your manners, Dominic. You're not too old to be taken over my knee.'

Dominic's eyebrow raised. At six feet, Dominic knew that his father knew his statement was ludicrous. He'd said it to disarm him and piss him off all at the same time. However, Dominic had had enough and he was eager to have this visit over and done with.

'Dad, tell me why you're here so I can enjoy the last of my weekend.'

'Willow, it was so lovely to meet you. I think that maybe you keep my son on his toes. He needs that. I can see he's also very protective of you.' Malcolm nodded and smiled. 'Good, good. Look after my boy.' Malcolm held her gaze until she followed suit and nodded back. 'Now, would you mind giving my son and me a few minutes? I want to have a quick catch-up.'

OUTPLAYED

'Sure, no problem. Dominic, I'm gonna go grab a seat over there,' she said indicating a free table not far from the bar.

'Thanks, Will. I won't be long.' He looked deep into her eyes, trying find any sign that she was disgusted by his interaction with his father. He couldn't see any, but that didn't necessarily mean it wasn't there. 'Do you want some wine?'

'That would be great.'

Dominic signalled Jamal over. 'Hey, let me get a glass of wine for Willow.' He knew Jamal didn't need to be told which one. She'd come to the bar enough for all the staff to know which wine she liked. 'And stick these in the back somewhere, will you,' he said, passing their overnight bag and helmets to him. Dominic didn't give his attention to his father until Willow had received her drink, walked over to the table and was fully settled with her phone in her hand and the wine glass to her beautiful lips.

⭐

Willow glanced at them covertly over her wine glass. To say she was in shock after meeting Malcolm Made was an understatement. Everything about him spoke of charm on steroids. But there was definitely something else that had the hairs on her arms standing up. That, coupled with Dominic's obvious disdain for the man, let Willow know that there was a story there to be told. She hoped one day Dominic would feel comfortable enough to share it with her.

She sipped on her wine, answered a message from Gabriela, who wanted to meet up and discuss some final preparations for the grand opening of *La Mesa Duquesa*, and kept a keen eye on Dominic and his father. Though she couldn't hear them, there wasn't a doubt in her mind that there were hostile words passing between them, or, at least, from Dominic to Malcolm. She didn't like seeing him like this, not even a little.

They spoke for no longer than fifteen minutes. Then they both got up from their respective barstools and just as Malcolm attempted to make a beeline for her, Dominic's outstretched arm blocking his advance convinced him that that would be an error. In the end, Malcolm simply waved at her and then headed out the door. Picking up a glass of what she was sure to be special bourbon, Dominic made his way over to her. The strain of the meeting was written all over his face and body language.

Dominic dropped into the chair beside her. 'Will, I'm so sorry you had to be subject to all of my family drama.'

'Don't worry about it. Who hasn't got drama?' She took a sip of her wine. 'Do you want to talk about it? I mean, you don't have to if you don't want to. But I'm here for you if you do want to.'

He smiled, but it didn't reach his eyes. He took a long swig of his drink before turning to her. 'He wanted money.'

'Money!' She couldn't keep the shock out of her voice.

'Yeah. He gave me some of the money to open this place. At the time, he said it was a gift to make up for past and numerous transgressions as a parent. Then, early on the day you and I first met, he came here asking me to return his "*gift*" after already spending days doing the same by text. So you see we were *both* in a foul mood that night.'

She took that all in and wondered what kind of a father would gift his child cash to open his dream business and then suddenly ask for it back years later.

OUTPLAYED

'I didn't have it all liquid at the time. But over the last few weeks, I've made a few business moves which have allowed me to give him back every last ill-gotten penny.'

She saw his knuckles tighten around his glass.

'Now, the man has the audacity to show up here asking for a loan. And big surprise, it's all for the same reason. Debts! Gambling ones to be precise. He owes people, loan sharks and the like. He gave me the money back when he was on a winning streak, which of course, I was unaware of. I guess this time the house is winning again.'

Willow's eyes widened. 'And are you going to give it to him?'

'Not a chance. When Joy and I were kids, the man pretty much gambled us out of house and home. He put our family through hell. The man was a yo-yo gambler and our mother always forgave him when he came back with his pathetic apologies. When he gave me the money to help me get this place off the ground, he said that it was his way of saying he's sorry for practically putting my mother into an early grave. To put the past behind us, I took it. I got the bar set up and thankfully it was popular. For a while, it seemed he'd turned his life around. He came by and helped out every now and then. But inevitably, he started spiralling again and then I told him to stop coming here. He did, until the day he asked for his "*gift*" back.'

'Oh, Dominic... I'm so sorry. I wish you hadn't had to go through all of that.'

He leaned in and gave her a peck on the lips. 'It's okay. The first day he actually came by here to ask for it back ended unexpectedly well, remember. A beautiful woman walked into my bar, assaulted my customer and then stole my heart on her way out. She's a menace. Someone should put her in her place.' He grinned.

Her heart skipped a beat and she got goosebumps, for a good reason this time. And it was at that moment she knew that this was the right time. Even if she wanted to, she knew her heart would no longer allow her to keep how she truly felt from this man.

'Dominic... I... love you.'

His grin grew wider. 'I know, baby. I've known for a while. But I'm so happy to hear you say the words for yourself. I love you too.'

For the first time in, she didn't know how many years, Willow felt at peace. Without warning, she felt herself start to tear up.

'Don't cry, my love,' he said as he wiped a tear that rolled down her cheek. 'This is a good thing.'

'I know,' she sniffed. 'Feeling this still scares me a little bit. But I think... I know I can trust you.'

He took her face between his hands. 'Yes, you can. *I would never hurt you*. At least, not like *he* did.'

They both knew which *'he'* Dominic was referring to. There was no need to bring the name of the object of Willow's ire into this conversation.

'I promise you now, Willow, I will spend the rest of my life keeping that smile on your beautiful face.'

She laughed and then planted a kiss on his waiting lips. She followed with her tongue, which he willingly accepted. Neither of them cared much about where they were at that moment. All that mattered was each other and all that they would share.

OUTPLAYED

'Am I gonna have to get the hose?' came the amused voice of Jamal.

Pausing from practically sucking each other's face off, both Dominic and Willow had the decency to look ashamed.

Dominic cleared his throat. 'Hey.'

Jamal smirked and shook his head. 'You want more drinks? Or are you two lovebirds all set?'

Willow giggled and spoke under her breath. '"*Lovebirds*"? How apt.'

'What was that?' Jamal asked.

'Oh, nothing.' Willow smiled. 'I'll have another. It's not a school night for me. Being unemployed has its advantages.'

'Not for long, soon-to-be restaurant manager,' Dominic pointed out.

'When you're right, you're right.'

'Another for me too, Jamal.'

Jamal nodded, turned on his heel and headed back to the bar. Glancing around, Willow could see that since they'd got back from their weekend away, the busyness of the bar had died down. It was closing time soon.

'If it didn't mean we'd get arrested for public indecency, I'd strip you down right here and replay our first time together,' he whispered gruffly in her ear.

At his guttural words, Willow turned to him. She looked into the deep pools of his grey eyes and saw that he meant every word he'd said.

'For you, I'd risk it.' She was only half joking. In that moment, she realised that she would do almost anything for Dominic. Because she loved him – truly, madly, deeply!

SHONEL JACKSON

After another couple of drinks and more sexual innuendos on steroids from Dominic, Bar Made was closed and the staff gone. He was in the office locking away the evening's takings and closing out the books for the night. Willow was alone now in the dimly lit bar area which was illuminated only by the blue glow of the fish tank. She stared transfixed as each of the tropical fish sliced through the water, leaving a swirl in their wake. She was so absorbed by their display that she didn't hear Dominic's approach, and she only knew when he encircled her around her waist. She sank into him, fully letting go of everything, every tiny voice in her head that made her afraid of getting hurt again, everything that stopped her from seeing what was right in front of her. Dominic was a good, kind, loving man who'd proven from the very first time they met that he saw her, *really* saw her. He'd showed her that if any potential harm was near her, whether it be to her heart or her person, he'd be right their ready to do battle for her. She no longer doubted him... nor herself, for that matter. It was now or never. She had to tell him everything.

'Dominic?'

'Hm.' He sounded like he was in a dreamy state.

'I need to tell you something.' She tried to not make her voice sound ominous, but she couldn't help it. She felt him tense and then she turned in his arms and looked up at him. 'Don't look so worried, my love. It's not about us. I just need to tell you some things.'

Dominic held her eyes for a beat, saying nothing. A small smile came to his lips, but it was gone so fast that she thought she might have imagined it, along with a brief look of relief in his eyes. Not relief that whatever she had to say was bad for them, but relief that she was finally about to let the last of her armour fall.

★

Dominic led her into the lift that would take them up to his apartment. 'You want something to drink?' he asked as he closed the front door behind them.

'Just water. I'm still slightly tipsy from all the wine.'

Dominic had never known Willow to be shy, but the wobble in her voice was unmistakable. He was in and out of his kitchen with a glass of water in under thirty seconds. He could tell that whatever she had to say to him was not going to be easy for her, but they both knew she had to get it out. He was positive that this would be the final piece of the dark puzzle that was Willow's life before he met her that night. She sat down on the sofa, curling her legs under her. He joined her there too, but angled his body so that he could look at her.

'When I found out that my ex was cheating on me, I kinda lost my mind. I mean, our marriage wasn't perfect, but I never imagined that he would do something like that to me. It was like the life I dreamed of for so long with a husband and babies had just vanished into thin air.'

She glanced over at him, and the tears he saw in her eyes nearly broke his heart. Even though he wanted to remove the distance between them, he decided to continue to give her space.

'You see, back then, we used to have the same style of phone. One morning, he forgot his at home. I was going to head into work later than normal as I had an appointment with my doctor... my fertility doctor.' She took in a gulp of air. 'I heard a text notification and, thinking it was my phone,

I picked it up from the bedside table.' She frowned as she continued. 'What I saw nearly made me sick. It was a photo of a woman's naked breasts plus a message below it. It said, "I can't wait to get these around you again, *Lesma*." At first, I thought it was some kind of porn spam or something as there was no name attached to the sender. But then it hit me that the person had used his Capoeira nickname in their message. It wasn't like it was a common name or anything, so of course he must have known the person. I realised that it was someone from the Capoeira world sending that to him. *From my world!* I saw red. I wanted to know who it was, so I decided I would call the number, but from my own phone instead. I typed the number into my phone and a name came up. I didn't need to call the number to find out who it was sending nudes to my husband. Apparently, it was someone I knew enough to have their contact details saved.'

Dominic was beginning to see red himself. It made him wish he'd done violence to the man the day he saw him at the Notting Hill Carnival Capoeira event.

'Seeing Priscilla's name come up as the owner of the number nearly killed me. She was my friend. She listened to me so many times go on and on about how we were struggling to conceive. I'd cried on her shoulder and she'd wiped away my tears... only to find out she'd been fucking my husband all along!' She made eye contact with him. 'I was in hell.'

It was breaking his heart knowing that she'd been through such pain, but he also knew she needed to get this out. 'I'm so sorry this happened to you, Will. I wish I could take away your pain.'

OUTPLAYED

'It gets worse,' she continued. 'I didn't confront him when I went to work. Later that evening, there was a class. Holding on to the knowledge of what they'd done to me all day had me fuming by evening. I went to class and my rage manifested itself in the worse possible way. I played Priscilla in the *roda* and I lost my shit. I didn't hold back. I played her aggressively and she got injured.' Willow choked up and buried her face in her hands.

It was at this point that he went over to her and pulled her into his arms. 'It's alright, let it out.'

'I'm so ashamed of myself. Never in my life had I played with such unrestrained fury. We were both on a par with each other in terms of Capoeira level, but I really wasn't myself that night. I caught her with a kick called a *chapa* straight to her chest, which normally, she'd have been able to escape. Even though I could see that she didn't have enough recovery time from a previous move of mine to escape the *chapa*, I still gave it to her with full force. I could have just tapped her with my foot if I wanted to, you know, to show her that I had her... the way we normally do in our school, but I guess vengeance took over that night.'

'Honey, as you said, she was equally as experienced as you. It sounds like she was off her game that night. It sounds to me like you just outplayed her.'

'Yes, I did outplay her, but I did it in a way that I wasn't proud of that night. When she recovered from the *chapa*, I went for her again. I caught her in a *tesouro*, which is a scissors takedown. I caught both of her legs tightly in between mine and then twisted over. This caused her to fall back. I did it so fast that she fell back and hit the back of her hard. The

Capoeira *roda* isn't for retaliation.' She shook her head. 'To this day, I can't believe I went that far. I have always been taught that Capoeira is to be used as a defence, not as an attack. I shamed myself and my school. After that, I never wanted to see either of them again. Not even myself sometimes when I looked into the mirror.

'I let him convince me to do couple's counselling and some other shit. Then I found out he'd never actually stopped sleeping with her. So, I left my school and moved down to London. Much later, when I felt myself again, I found *Jogo Arrepiado Capoeira*. Needless to say, I wasn't very open with the other students I met there, especially with Gabriela. She tried so hard to include me in events and welcome me, but I was still pretty bruised from the last time I had a good friend in a Capoeira school.' She finally smiled. 'She was so good to me and didn't give up on me. She pulled me out of my funk. And now she's given me a career again. I don't think I'll ever be able to show her the extent of my gratitude.'

Dominic looked at her with new eyes. 'Willow, you're amazing, you know that?'

She raised one eyebrow and looked at him quizzically. 'Why? Because I can become volatile when pushed?'

He laughed. 'No, not that. What I mean is, after everything you went through, all the trust you lost in people... now you're here, out on the other side *and* you've let this roughish, Harley-riding, bar owner into your life... I admire that.'

She rolled her eyes. '*Roughish?* That's not quite the adjective I would use to describe you, Mr. Made.'

He raised his eyebrow. 'Oh? And what adjective *would* you use, Miss Blake?'

OUTPLAYED

She smiled and placed her hand on his chest over his heart. 'Well, there are many. I'll give you a few... kind, understanding, non-judgemental and loving.'

He was choked up by her words.

'Oh, yeah... and *sexy as hell!*'

He cracked up. 'You flatter me, Willow. Does this mean that you see me as a piece of meat?'

She sobered. 'You're everything to me, Dominic. And I'm so glad that on one night in a truly awful week, I needed a drink and wandered into your bar. Thank you.'

'You don't need to thank me. I love you. Now, would you please kiss me?'

'My pleasure,' she said with a smile before she jumped him.

The kiss that she laid on him after she straddled him had Dominic's head in a daze. The feeling of her tongue plunging into his mouth sent shockwaves up his spine and straight down to his cock. With a grunt, he dragged her up and she proceeded to jump up and wrap her strong legs around his waist. He held onto her arse firmly to support her and gladly accepted her hot tongue once more. Using nothing but his muscle memory, because it certainly wasn't his eyes, he found his way to his bedroom before placing her down on her feet.

'Strip!' This was an order from him, not a request. And, from the hot look in her brown eyes, he knew he wouldn't have to say it twice. He watched as she seductively peeled away every layer. He'd seen her naked many times, but this time, it was different. Seeing her on display like this with not a hint of uncertainty in her eyes, after hearing her finally tell him that she loved him, made this a very different moment entirely.

Without breaking eye contact with her, he began to slowly strip for her too. He watched her as she watched him and it made him harder by the second. She then surprised him. As soon as he stepped out of his boxers, she came to him and dropped to her knees in front of him. He had barely taken a breath before she sucked it right back out of him as she took him into her mouth.

'*Wil—low...*' He was convinced that her name wasn't audible when he spoke. He knew that he'd spoken, but his own voice sounded distant and alien to him. He threw his head back and savoured the moment. His eyes rolled back into his head as he gave himself over to her completely. She gripped his shaft and pounded, woodpecker-like, around his cock. It was the single most erotic moment of his life. The fact that she was his... *his* woman... the love of his life... well, someone could have knocked him over with a feather, he was so high.

She swirled and licked her tongue all over his tip and sucked up every drop of his precum. When he felt himself hit the back of her throat, he thought that was when he would lose it.

'*Baby...*' To his own ears, he sounded drunk. 'If you don't want this to come to an abrupt end, you're gonna have to stop right now.'

All she did was look up at him, mouth full of dick, and wink at him slyly. He could see that she had no intention of listening to him. It took everything he had to put an end to what she was doing and draw her sexy arse up from her ministrations.

'Okay, you little minx, my turn.' He turned her around and bent her over so that her upper body lay on the bed. Then it was his turn to assume the position. He tilted her hips and spread her cheeks. When his tongue came into contact with her already soaked lips, she let out an ear piecing scream. For the next while, he took his time as his tongue and lips went on a mission of exploration. With every thrust and suck and lap, she groaned in pleasure as she pushed her hips backwards. He revelled in this as he let one and then two of his fingers have a go. He felt her shudder when the second one went in and that's when he knew he had her just where he wanted her.

'Come for me, baby. That's right, let go. Just let go...'

She tightened around his fingers as her orgasm took hold of her, but he didn't let up. He continued to plunder her as her creamy liquid spilled out and coated his fingers. When her shudders finally subsided, he got up and went to his en suite to get a damp wash cloth to clean her up. When he re-entered the room, she hadn't moved, but he could see that she was teetering on the edge and could crumble to the floor at any time.

'Woah, baby... come, let me help you.' After cleaning her up, he helped her to find her way to properly lie on the bed.

Fuck me, Dominic! That was... that was... I have no words...'

He grinned as he kneeled above her on the bed. 'Your wish is my command, Miss Blake.' He sheathed himself, spread her legs, then eased his throbbing cock into her welcoming folds. He kept his eyes pinned to her face as she succumbed to more pleasure.

'Baby... love you so much,' she said on a pant.

'Love you too, beautiful. Love you forever.'

Dominic knew that this time, he could not be gentle. The beast inside him was on feral mode, so he pumped and pumped and drove into her until, with a final gasp of exhilaration, he shot his hot load deep inside her quaking core. He'd kept going as long as he could because there was no way he was going to come if she wasn't right there with him. She came violently with his name on her lips and he knew that he was a luckiest S.O.B. to have this beautiful woman under him and, even better, in love with his undeserving arse.

EPILOGUE

- bateria -

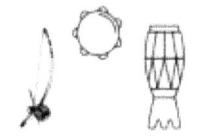

It was opening night of *La Mesa Duquesa* and the place was packed. Willow and Gabriela had spent the last couple of weeks putting the finishing touches on everything... the decorations, the menu, the tastings, the promo, the RSVPs, the press... No stone had gone unturned to make this opening something to behold.

The buzz about the place had been electric. They had a three-month waiting list before they'd even served a plate. This opening night though was mostly filled with family and friends along with V.I.P. members and regulars from Gabriela's nightclub, *La Duquesa*. A large contingent of the diners were from *Jogo Arrepiado Capoeira*. Some of them had flown in from as far afield as Germany, Sweden and Brazil to be here.

Gabriela looked around the well-lit, vibrant restaurant. Seeing the smiles on the faces of her family and friends made her heart feel full. Her father couldn't stop telling her how proud he was of her that she'd taken the night club, which he'd handed over to her years ago, and made it bigger and better than he could have ever imagined. He'd told her that her mother was smiling down on her and would be overjoyed to see how she'd expanded the family business into a brand. '*La marca Duquesa*,' he'd said. From the head of the main table in the busy restaurant, Gabriela glanced to her left to see her bestie, Luna, and Luna's handsome husband, Javier. They had flown in from Spain to be here for this. Even after Luna had left their Capoeira school and moved to Spain to be with the man she loved and raise her beautiful daughter Lexi, they'd remained close. Javier's family vineyard was also *La Mesa Duquesa's* primary wine supplier. Their winery, *La Bodega Martínez*, produced excellent wine and she couldn't wait for her future customers to fall in love with it as much as she had. Gabriela smiled once more. She truly did feel blessed.

✦

Luna looked around *La Mesa Duquesa*. There were no words for how proud she was of her friend Gabriela. One of her hands squeezed her husband Javier's thigh with excitement. As he was her big, strong now Capoeira *mestre*, she knew he could take it. There were so many familiar faces around her whom she missed tremendously now that she lived in Spain. The people from her old Capoeira school here in London were like a family to her. Even though her life was in another place, nothing would change that. Now, there was a new member of her martial arts family. She'd only been back a week or so, but she'd spent a lot of time with Willow. Luna remembered how Gabriela had first described her. She'd said Willow pretty much kept them all at arm's length and wasn't really up for joining in with any of the social events outside of class. Luna was happy to see the transformation. The three of them and their men had had dinner at Gabriela's house one night this week, had quite a few adult beverages at Dominic's bar another night and torn up the Capoeira *roda* in between. Even though Dominic didn't play, he'd still tagged along and lent his voice to the game. In the short time since they'd met, Luna knew that she liked Willow. They'd exchanged numbers and there were already preliminary plans for the two London-based couples to come spend some time at their family home and vineyard in Spain. Luna smiled. She felt lucky to have so many friends like the ones she saw around her now.

⭐

Willow looked around the hectic kitchen. The Cuban cuisine was flying out to the diners, especially the *ropa vieja*. She felt a lot of pressure as it was opening night and her skills to lead this team of employees would be tested. Most of all, she didn't want to disappoint Gabriela. They were now very close friends, but she always wanted to give her all on the professional front.

When she was satisfied that she wasn't needed, she headed back out into the dining area. She cast her eyes around and felt excitement for the turnout they had. There were no empty seats in the place. Well, except for the one at the main table, which was hers. Though she was dining with her friends, she was still the newbie manager and she felt compelled to make sure everything was running smoothly. So, every few minutes, she got up from the table to check one thing or the other. Even though Gabriela had insisted that she sit and that everything was going fine, Willow couldn't help herself. She wanted to judge for herself.

When she was finally satisfied that the place wouldn't crumple without her meticulous supervision, she finally dropped down on the chair next to her love. 'Okay, I'm back.'

'Finally! You were missing all the toasts,' Dominic said. 'You know your friends are crazy, right?'

Willow laughed. 'Yep! They're the best friends a girl could ask for.'

'Hey, Willow!' Gabriela shouted across the table to her. 'How's my restaurant doing?'

'Running like a well-oiled machine, boss lady,' Willow said with a wink.

'That's what I like to hear.' Gabriela raised her champagne glass to Willow. 'Here's to the best damn manager a girl could ask for. For all that you've done, above and beyond, over the last few weeks, to make sure this night went off without a hitch... Willow... I thank you. *Del fundo de mi corazón*... from the bottom of my heart.' Gabriela placed her palm over her heart.

The moisture in Gabriela's eyes as she spoke had Willow tearing up too. She sent a kiss to Gabriela over the table. 'You deserve it, hun, and more. Your friendship has meant the world to me. You'll forever have my gratitude and love.'

⭐

Long after all the champagne had been drunk and the grand opening of *La Mesa Duquesa* had ended, Dominic and Willow lay in bed spooning. Dominic gently caressed her bare thigh as she rambled on about how the night had gone.

'...gosh, babe, everything went so well... so much great feedback from everyone... and did you see Gabriela... and Luna... she's so cool too...'

OUTPLAYED

On and on she went, but Dominic didn't mind one bit. Willow was his woman and she was happy, and that was all that mattered.

Happy wife, happy life... right?

The moment the thought formed in Dominic's mind, his eyes widened and a smile formed on his lips. Willow, of course, wasn't in his head and couldn't see his face, so he was free to let his thoughts take him wherever they wanted to go as he lovingly stroked her thigh. In just a few seconds he saw his entire future before his eyes. Willow in a sexy white dress, a honeymoon on an exotic beach somewhere, exploring and re-exploring every single inch of this beautiful body of hers and then one day, when they were ready, welcoming a son or daughter into this world... a child who'd be the perfect mix of both of them... his drive and determination... her feistiness and beauty. These were picture-perfect moments in his mind.

'A man can dream...' he said quietly to himself. He had zoned out of what she was saying and hadn't realised he'd spoken out loud.

'What was that, baby? What about dreams?' she asked as she turned around and eyed him curiously.

He smiled mysteriously and looked piercingly into the deep pools of her eyes. 'Oh, nothing... just that I like it when people's dreams come true. Who knows? I think a few more will come true before long.'

'You know what, babe... I couldn't agree with you more if I tried,' she said as she smiled at him in a 'come hither' way while walking her finger nails up his chiselled chest. 'I predict mine are going to be coming true right... this... second...'

SHONEL JACKSON

THE END

Don't miss out!

Visit the website below and you can sign up to receive emails whenever Shonel Jackson publishes a new book. There's no charge and no obligation.

https://books2read.com/r/B-A-PMXX-IMSBG

BOOKS 2 READ

Connecting independent readers to independent writers.

Did you love *Outplayed*? Then you should read *Let's Play*[1] by Shonel Jackson!

Gabriela Espinosa is no 007!

Let's get that straight! What she is, is the owner of *La Duquesa*, a high end night club in the Centre of London. In Book 1 of the *Era Capoeira* series, she meets a man one night who will ignite her passions. The meeting happens quite by accident... because she is spying! As *Let's Play* begins, Gabriela is called by the rich, often sensual music of *Capoeira*. If she hadn't been in the right place at the right time, they might never have met. But from the moment they first lay eyes on

---

1. https://books2read.com/u/bPLxVz

2. https://books2read.com/u/bPLxVz

each other, the spell was cast...Sean Lancaster is a successful hotelier in the prime of his life. His business is growing leaps and bounds and his life has been enriched by *Capoeira*, a martial art which he has loved since he was a teenager. He has no complaints. But one night, a chance encounter with a stunningly intoxicating woman has Sean realising that maybe there is something missing in his perfect life.He just had to hope that after he gives her a business card, she actually contacts him.

Read more at https://www.shoneljackson.com/.

About the Author

Shonel is originally from Guyana in South America. She moved to London as a teenager. She's a creative by nature and has been a professional actress, poet, an English as a foreign teacher and jewellery design/maker.

She fell in love with romance novels as a teenager. Throughout her life, she's consumed them ravenously. She started writing her own a few years after reading her first. Nothing could stop her after that.

She loves to write strong female leads, primarily women of colour. Her ladies are vibrant, worldly and not afraid of a challenge. Her guys are irresistible and smouldering and will stop at nothing to win their prize.

You'll laugh, maybe shed a little tear and drown in the worlds she likes to weave.

Read more at www.shoneljackson.com.